"I don't believe how good you look soaking wet."

January's T-shirt was clinging to her skin, her breasts outlined in sharp relief. She didn't move as Lance walked toward her and, putting his hands on her shoulders, began to kiss her. Instead of pushing him away, she found her arms went around him, pulling herself closer against him, the warmth of his bare chest penetrating the wet T-shirt. His mouth against hers seemed to take possession of her whole being. He kissed her cheeks, her eyelids, the side of her neck, and whispered in her ear, as his arms tightened around her, "You are so beautiful, January..."

Dear Reader,

Your enthusiastic reception of SECOND CHANCE
AT LOVE has inspired all of us who work on this
special romance line and we thank you.

Now there are *six* brand new, exciting SECOND
CHANCE AT LOVE romances for you each month.
We've doubled the number of love stories in our line
because so many readers like you asked us to. So, you
see, your opinions, your ideas, what you think, really
count! Feel free to drop me a note to let me know your
reactions to our stories.

Again, thanks for so warmly welcoming SECOND
CHANCE AT LOVE and, please, *do* let me hear
from *you*!

With every good wish,

Carolyn Nichols

Carolyn Nichols
SECOND CHANCE AT LOVE
The Berkley/Jove Publishing Group
200 Madison Avenue
New York, New York 10016

HEARTTHROB
MARGARETT McKEAN

SECOND CHANCE AT LOVE BOOK

chapter

1

JANUARY signed her name a final time to the divorce papers and sat back with a sigh of satisfaction. At last it was over. Never again would she be called Mrs. Michael Stone. From now on it was her own name, January Warburton, the by-line that had always gone on her articles and photos. She might have once been madly in love with Mike Stone, but that had ended more than eighteen months ago when it turned out that all the ugly rumors printed in the gossip columns were true. Mike *was* having an affair with that little platinum-blonde.

Rule number one, she thought, don't get involved with people in the music business. Which wasn't easy to avoid doing, she reminded herself wryly, when that was where one worked. Speaking of work . . . she picked up the red pencil and went through her own article one more time.

A quick rap on the smoked-glass door of her office made her look up. She smiled as, without waiting for her nod, Adrian Davis slid the door open and strode in. He lowered his long, angular body into the modern tubular steel chair across from her and tossed a folder on her desk. Adrian, as editor and owner of *Offbeat Magazine,* made himself at home in all the offices.

January smiled cheerfully at her boss. "To what do I owe this honor?"

Adrian squinted his blue eyes at her. "You're looking exceptionally beautiful today."

January tugged at her luxurious dark hair. She knew the soft lavender shade of her silk blouse accented her tan and highlighted the violet of her long-lashed eyes. As a photojournalist for Los Angeles's most prestigious music magazine, January realized it was important that she look well. That she managed to do so with minimal make-up and hairstyling was due to her natural beauty and the regimen of good health and excercise she insisted on.

"Thanks for the compliment," she said to Adrian, "but surely that's not what you came to say?"

"Nope." His ever-observant eye spotted the thick envelope on her desk. "What's that?"

"Divorce papers. Signed, sealed, and done."

"So you're a free woman again." Adrian's voice was sympathetic. "How's it feel?"

"Fine," January said. "Just fine." Her words faltered a bit. Hastily she smiled. "And I will thank you in the future to not fix me up with any more music producers."

Adrian winked. "I never told you to marry him. Dinner and an interview was all I said. The rest of the mistakes were yours."

"I concede," January said quickly. "You told me Michael could never stick with one woman and you were right."

"Do I detect a note of bitterness?"

"Bitter only that I was too young and foolish to listen. I'll know better next time."

"Aha," Adrian said. "Then you are finally open to the idea of a next time."

"Adrian, did you come in here to discuss my personal life or business?"

"Both, of course. Don't avoid the question."

January shifted in her chair so she could look out the window. The view of Los Angeles from the top floor of the Sunset Boulevard highrise was spectacular. "My work is enough for me right now," she said. "I don't want to get involved again, Adrian. Not for a long time. If there is a next time, it has to be good. I wonder sometimes if you realize how lucky you and Alicia are. You two have one of the best marriages I know."

"It's not all luck," Adrian said softly. "It's work, too. You can't stay buried away forever, January. Your divorce papers may have just come through, but you and Make separated over eighteen months ago. You've dated no one. If nothing else, my dear, there are some healthy bodily urges that cannot be ignored. You must be feeling them."

January blushed slightly.

Adrian went on. "To say nothing of the need for comfort, affection, and companionship that we all have."

"I'm not ready yet. It's that simple. But I appreciate the concern." And she did. January was twenty-five and had been on her own since she was nineteen. Although Adrian was only forty, he and his wife, Alicia, had taken a sort of parental interest in her since she'd come to work for *Offbeat* four years ago. It was good to know people cared.

"Okay," said January, "enough of my personal life. What's up?"

"I've got an assignment for you," said Adrian. "I want you to go on the road."

January brightened. "Cover story?"

"Series of articles. Lead features on L. A. Expressway."

"The hot new band?"

"Hot, yes. New, no. They're a California group who've been around for a while. They have a good following here on the West Coast but not so big in the east. Their new album is coming out soon and Platinum Records is setting up a promotional tour for them. I want you to go with them."

"Photos, interviews, the works?"

"Exactly," said Adrian. "I've already arranged it with their producer, Jay Livingston. They called today to tell me Lance approved the idea."

"Lance?"

"Lance Devlin, the lead singer and driving force behind the band."

"When do they leave?" January asked.

"About a week."

"Awfully short notice, isn't it?"

Adrian nodded. "Here's even shorter notice for you— I need two cover stories on Lance and L. A. Expressway by Monday noon."

"Adrian, you're crazy!" January gasped. "It's Thursday. The paper is put to bed this evening and is on the stands a week from today. We've already done the cover stories—they're set and ready to go."

"I've canceled them. We'll hold them for the next issue. This issue's going to Lance Devlin. The center pages and cover photo will be done by you and Steve Creighton this weekend."

"Creighton?" January said. "Why him? He has the mentality and style of a gossip columnist."

"Steve is also associate editor along with you. You just don't like his attitude toward women," Adrian said.

"I don't like his attitude, period," she replied.

Adrian shrugged. "We've been through this a hundred times. At any rate, you and Steve are handling these stories, and Steve has final okay on the cover design and inside copy for this issue."

"Why? Where are you going to be?" January asked.

"In Chicago. Covering the Rolling Stones concert."

"You sure are giving me a lot of last minute information today," January said. "Since when did you cover concerts?"

"Since Mick Jagger agreed to give me that long-awaited interview." Adrian grinned.

"Terrific," January said sarcastically. "You get Mick Jagger and I get Lance Devlin. Thanks a lot. What's he like, anyway? Devlin, I mean."

Adrian reached into the folder he'd thrown on her desk and pulled out an eight-by-ten glossy. He handed it to January.

Bold eyes seemed to wink mockingly out of the black-and-white picture. The shot was a close-up of the lead singer. His hair was light, falling softly around his ears and over his forehead. His cheekbones were high, his skin clear. His mouth was soft, sensuous, on the edge of laughter. Only the hard jawline indicated the strong stubborn streak January was somehow sure he had.

"Good looking, isn't he?" Adrian said.

January dropped the photo on her desk hastily, realizing she'd been staring hard at it since the instant Adrian had put it into her hands. "Not bad," she said. "How's his music?"

"Good." Adrian handed her another picture, one of the whole group together.

Lance was wearing leather pants, a white shirt open to the waist. His body looked lean and hard. The rest of the group was similarly dressed. January liked their looks: rough, but orderly. They appeared professional. "Who's the girl?" she asked casually, pointing to the long-haired woman at the mike beside Lance.

"That's Teri. She sings harmonies. Beautiful voice—sounds a little like Carly Simon. She's married to Joel, the piano player. That's Derek on bass, and Samson on drums."

"What's their sound?" January asked, pushing the pictures of Lance away from her. It had been a long time since she'd seen a man she found so attractive, and the last thing she needed was to be attracted to a man she was about to go on the road with, especially a musician. She knew all she wanted to know—and then some—about musicians.

"Sort of a cross between Fleetwood Mac and the Eagles," he said, "if you can imagine it."

Years of working with Adrian enabled January to imagine it easily. L.A. Expressway's sound would be easy rock with good harmonies and guitar work; some slow ballads, some fast numbers. She wondered if they had anything to distinguish them from all the other bands producing just those sounds. She assumed they must or Adrian wouldn't be taking such an interest in them. Adrian had an almost infallible ability to determine who was going to make it and who wasn't.

"When do I meet them?" January asked.

Adrian glanced at his watch. "Any minute now. I told Lance to come by the office. I thought you two could have lunch together."

January grinned. "Oh you did, did you?"

The voice of *Offbeat*'s receptionist came over the speaker on January's desk: "Lance Devlin here to see you."

Adrian winked. "Take him somewhere nice. He likes to eat well." He unfolded himself from the chair and walked to the door.

"Hey," said January, "aren't you even going to introduce us?"

But Adrian was already gone.

Typical, thought January, and then said into the intercom, "Tell Mr. Devlin, I'll be right with him." Hastily she pulled open her desk drawer, pulled out a mirror, checked her face, and ran a comb through her long dark hair. Come on, Warburton, she said to herself, dropping the mirror back in the drawer. What are you doing? It's just one more rock star. She pushed the drawer shut and glanced again at the pictures Adrian had left on her desk. If he looked anything like his pictures, she thought with a smile . . .

She was about to tell the receptionist to send Devlin in when the door slid open and Lance Devlin himself sauntered into her office.

January felt a shock go through her. He was even better looking than his photos. She picked up her phone, pressing a button so that the receptionist's voice could not be heard over the speaker. "Helen, I thought I said..."

"I know, Ms. Warburton, but he just pushed right past me..."

"Okay," said January, "never mind. I'll handle it."

Lance was leaning against the door, hands in the pockets of his blue jeans, a lazy grin on his face.

January fought an impulse to throw him out of her office. She reminded herself she was going to be practically living with him and his band for at least a month— unless she told Adrian to give the job to someone else.

"Have a seat," she said politely. "I'm January Warburton, and you're..." She held out her hand.

He ignored her hand and slid down into the chair Adrian had vacated. "Lance Devlin, as if you didn't know. You have my pictures right there in front of you."

"Are you always so polite?" she said sarcastically.

"I hate to be kept waiting," he said easily. "And I hate the press."

"Then what are you doing here?" January snapped.

Lance grinned. "I need you. *Offbeat*'s the best music rag in the country and we could use the publicity. You people need us because we're about to be the hottest group around."

"If that's true," January retorted, "then you don't need anyone. Good music creates its own publicity."

"True," he said, "but a little advance promotion never hurt anyone."

"Calculating, aren't you?"

"How do you think I've survived in this business so long? It's dog eat dog. You ought to know. It's papers like yours that have everyone slitting each other's throats. You just love to keep the competition going, don't you?"

"Any more hostility you care to vent on me?" she asked evenly.

"Not for the moment." Lance lounged back in the chair, lifted his long legs, and eased his booted feet down onto her desk top.

"Take your feet off my desk," January said softly. She didn't know why she said it. Adrian sat with his feet on her desk all the time.

He put his feet down. "Excu—uu—se me," he said in a Steve Martin imitation. "Mind if I smoke?"

January pushed an ashtray toward him.

"Never mind," he said, "just testing. I don't smoke. Bad for the throat."

"Are you always this obnoxious?"

"Usually," Lance said. "Especially with the press."

"Well, let me give you some advice," January said. "We're going to be spending quite a bit of time together. I'm going to be interviewing you and everyone in your band. I'll be writing about all your shows and doing all the photos. I am going to be covering your first major eastern tour. For all I know, you are just one more two-bit L.A. band with the same old worn out sounds of all the other bands. Then again, you might be good. But whatever you are, I'm going to report it straight. It would be to your advantage to make all the effort in the world you can to get along with me. Get it?"

"Got it," Lance said. "Now you get this, December or February or whatever your name is. I don't know you, and I don't like you. I don't like you because you have just admitted to me that you don't even know what my band sounds like. And you are about to go on the road with us. Typical press.

"All you want is your story. It doesn't matter to you what we sound like. You'll say anything you want just so long as it sells your paper. So don't talk to me about getting along. You know and I know that it doesn't matter a damn if we get along or not. I'll play my music; you'll write your garbage. You'll sell your paper, and hopefully we'll sell tickets to our concerts. As for 'getting along,' that's just the setup before the sellout, so don't give me that."

White-faced and furious, January stared at him. Seeing his arrogant green eyes, she knew there was no sense in telling him she hadn't had a chance to listen to his music because she'd only found out five minutes ago she was going on the road with his group. Tight-lipped, she said instead, "I will make a deal with you, Mr. Devlin. I will listen to your music. If I don't like it, I will not take this assignment. Someone else who does like your sound will be sent to cover the tour instead. Will that satisfy you? As for your music, if it's as hostile, as rude, as utterly contemptible as you are, I am sure I will loathe it. Now, get out of my office." January's normally soft violet eyes were almost black with anger. She stood up. "Out," she said.

Lance's eyes traveled slowly from January's set face to her trembling body, lingered a moment, then met her eyes again. He stood up also. "If you get someone else for the job," he said, "as I'm sure you will, get a guy. Women reporters are the worst."

It took all January's strength to resist hurling her dictionary at him as Lance ambled nonchalantly out of her office.

Conceited jerk, she thought, sitting back down, trying to stop her hands from shaking.

She pressed the button on the phone for Adrian's office.

"No way," she said when she got him, "am I going to work with that stupid, arrogant bastard. No way, Adrian. Get someone else." She slammed the receiver down.

Adrian was at her door in seconds. "What happened?"

"What didn't happen?" She told him the story. "We don't need him, Adrian, no matter how good he is," she concluded. "Believe me, he's not worth the hassle."

"Come on," said Adrian. "He can't be that bad."

"He's worse."

"You're edgy," Adrian said. "Divorce papers, no boyfriend, a sexy guy comes into your office, and you get all hot under the collar."

She glared at him.

"Okay, okay," he soothed, "calm down. If he's really that awful, we'll get someone else on the story. I wanted you because you're the best. No one on the staff can both write and photograph as well as you. If you don't go, it'll mean sending two people."

"Send Steve Creighton," January said. "Frankly, with the hostility he has toward the press, I think you're wasting your time sending anyone."

"I need Steve here." Adrian paused. "Aw, hell. You know you're the best at a story like Devlin and L. A. Expressway, so do me one favor. Keep your end of the bargain."

"What's that?"

"Listen to his music. If you really don't like it, then you're off the assignment. But if you do, then cover the tour. Deal?"

"Deal," January said, convinced that nothing on earth could make her like Lance Devlin and L. A. Expressway's music.

"There are some demo tapes on my desk. Go listen to them now. You can close the door and have the office to yourself. I'm going to lunch. I'll tell Helen not to let anyone disturb you."

"If I don't like it I'm off the story, right?"

"Right." Adrian grinned. "One thing I know for certain is that you'd never lie to me. If you like Devlin's music, you'll say so."

True, thought January, as she walked down the thickly carpeted corridor to Adrian's office. But one thing she knew for certain was that she wouldn't like Devlin's music.

She sat down at Adrian's desk. The tapes, reel to reel, were in square boxes. She picked one up, opened the box, took the clear plastic reel out and clicked it onto the large machine behind the desk. She pulled the brown tape through the magnetic heads and wound it onto the empty spool. Before pressing the on button, she read the notes on the box. The tape was a demo dub of a master for their first album.

"L. A. Expressway," she read, "*Diamonds of the Sea,* Side One." Okay, Devlin, she thought, let's see what you do.

First song, first side was the title song of the album, "Diamonds of the Sea." She pushed the on button, sat back in Adrian's chair, and closed her eyes to listen. Despite all that Lance had said one thing January was, was fair. She would listen to Devlin's music as if she had never heard of him or spoken to him in her life.

The first sounds were chimes, soft and silvery, followed by the opening guitar chords, minor chords. January relaxed. She loved the minor chords. Piano, bass, drums, each instrument entered slowly, picking up on and echoing the others. Rather, she thought, like waves of the ocean themselves, breaking one after the other, gently washing up onto the sand. A girl's voice came in. Teri, January realized, remembering the picture. Lance's voice followed last, coming in quietly, picking up on the melody and then taking over the whole song, carrying it. Something in Lance's voice struck a chord in January, seemed to touch her deep inside. It seemed impossible that the angry man she had seen earlier could sing so beautifully.

The song was a love song, lyrical, melodic, the words weaving fine poetic images. Finding real love, the song said, was as rare as finding diamonds in the sea. Wasn't that the truth, January thought ironically, and wondered who had written the song. She looked at the box. "All songs by Lance Devlin."

She pressed rewind and played the first song through again, this time forgetting everything, giving herself up to the music.

She had listened to the entire tape once and was halfway through a second time when Adrian walked in. So caught up was she in the music that she didn't hear him enter.

"Well?" he said.

His voice startled her and she sat up straight. A soft smile came on her face as she saw Adrian.

"Great," she said. "He's really great. His personality stinks, but his music is brilliant. I don't know how I'm ever going to get along with him, but it looks as if I'll have to find a way."

Adrian smiled. "I thought you'd feel that way."

"One thing you were wrong about, though," she said. "He's better, much better, than the groups you compared him to." She grinned. "I predict that L. A. Expressway will soon be the hottest group around." And then she groaned. "But how on earth am I ever going to get him to open up and trust me?"

"January, if you can't find a way no one can."

"Maybe I shouldn't take the assignment, Adrian. He hates women reporters."

"You can make him trust you," Adrian said. "Believe me, you're a perfect match."

To her total confusion, January found herself blushing.

"So you do like him after all," he said thoughtfully. "That's what all those sparks were about."

"I like him as a musician," January said, clicking off the tape recorder. "Business only, Adrian Davis, and don't try to turn it into anything else. Last time you did that, you almost destroyed my life."

Adrian grinned. "Not I, my dear—Mike Stone."

"Please don't mention the name. I just got rid of it today. What's Devlin's number? I better call and set up an interview."

Adrian handed her a piece of paper with the number on it. "If you're free tonight, come have dinner with Alicia and me."

"Thanks," said January, "that'd be nice. I get tired of my own cooking."

"You can't live alone forever, January. Sooner or later you're going to have to let someone into your life."

"Later," she said with a grin, "much later." She

glanced at the number. "Where does he live? Looks like a beach number."

"Malibu."

She nodded. "Figures. Well," she said, "here goes nothing. I'll call him."

"Let me know what happens," Adrian said. "Tonight at dinner. Eight o'clock."

January nodded and headed for her office. She handed the number to Helen as she passed by her desk. "Put a call through to Lance Devlin for me," she said.

Helen grimaced. "That charming man?"

"Exactly," January said.

Helen began pressing the buttons on her phone and January went into her office to wait.

Okay, Warburton, she said to herself, very very smooth. Somehow you have to get this guy to trust you.

Helen's voice came over the intercom. "Lance Devlin on the line."

January picked up the receiver. "Lance, January Warburton here."

chapter

2

SURFERS and swimmers lined the edge of the Pacific Coast Highway, their golden brown bodies leaning against vans and motorcycles. January envied them the luxury of having nothing to do but lie in the sun. She was not looking forward to this interview with Lance. He had been as cynical on the phone as he had been in her office. She rarely got a Saturday to herself and she'd been anticipating this one with pleasure. Not that she had had special plans. To wash her Volkswagen beetle and work in her flower garden outside her Laurel Canyon house had been about it. Instead, on this surprisingly hot mid-April Saturday afternoon, she was driving to Lance's house in Malibu.

He had said to bring a bathing suit, but for some perverse reason she had decided not to. Now she wished she had. A swim would be lovely, if not in Lance's pool, then at the beach on the way home.

His place was on Bluewater Road, an area known for its expensive houses, wide lawns, private beaches; an area inhabited by wealthy actors, producers and, of course, rock stars. Lance was living in style, January thought with a wry smile. A guard stopped her at the gate, found her name on a list, and let her in. It was a ritual January had grown accustomed to. Rock stars protected themselves more assiduously than politicians. She wondered as she drove up the paved driveway if Lance wasn't being a little premature. West Coast success wasn't national or international fame. He wasn't that popular or well known yet. She was surprised he could even afford the long, low, hacienda-style house she saw just ahead of her.

A number of cars were parked in front of the house. Behind it, hazy blue and sparkling with sunlight, stretched the Pacific Ocean. January took a deep breath of sea air as she closed the car door and walked up to the house. The lightweight crepe de chine sundress she wore swung easily around her legs. On her feet were thin sandals with narrow straps that tied around her ankles. She had caught her thick hair up on top of her head, leaving only a few tendrils to curl at the nape of her neck. In her oversized handwoven shoulder bag were a notebook, a small Sony cassette recorder, and a miniature Minolta.

There was no need to knock on the wide front door. It was already open. Evidently anyone who got past the guard was welcome to just wander into the house. And that was just as well because no one would have heard her knock over the music blasting throughout the house. She walked through the entryway that led to a large glassed in living room which opened onto the pool, and she saw the source—loudspeakers tucked into every possible nook and cranny.

And she saw bodies all over the place: sprawled on the off-white modular seating in the living room, lying

on the vast Oriental rug on the floor, half asleep on the
deck chairs outside, floating on air mattresses in the pool.
Lance was nowhere to be seen amongst them. Scarcely
anyone even bothered to look up as she walked through.
One long-haired, blue-jeaned young man held up his beer
to her. She shook her head. He shrugged and took a
swallow. A girl by the pool said, "Looking for a bathing
suit? There're lots in the house." Again January shook
her head.

She was in no great hurry to find Lance. She preferred
to have a glimpse of his lifestyle without him around.
It was a lifestyle apparently similar to that of many musicians she'd encountered. Along with their need to con-
stantly ensure their privacy, they had an incredible need
to be surrounded by hordes of people. Hangers-on, January thought. As if they were afraid to be alone. Inevitably the music would be blasting as it was now, beer
and liquor flowing freely. It was a scene she had never
much liked, and if it weren't for her great love of music
she wouldn't be around it.

She wandered down a long corridor hung with tapes-
tries and fine paintings. Incongruous, she thought. She
wondered whose taste in art it was. Lance's? It seemed
unlikely. A partially opened door led into a small den
filled with books. Probably all unread, she reflected hastily. There were no stereo speakers in the den. It was cool
and dark. She sank down on the leather couch. The den
reminded her of her own shady little house nestled into
the hillside amongst the trees. All that was needed now
was a little classical music.

As if someone had heard her thoughts, Schumann's
piano composition "Scenes from Childhood" came drift-
ing toward her. One of her favorite pieces of music, it
made her sit up and listen attentively, an expression of
delight in her eyes. She wondered where it was coming
from. Certainly not from the main speakers through
which rock music was still blasting away in other parts
of the house.

Across the room three steps led down to a door. Noise-

lessly, she walked over, went down the steps, and pushed
it open. Immediately the sounds of the piano grew louder.
She looked into the room. It was very large and equipped
for rehearsals. In the center, on a low platform, was a
set of drums. Leaning against the walls was an array of
electric guitars. There were mikes, cables, wires everywhere. And in one corner, by a large open window, with
sun streaming in and the sea beyond, was a beautiful
grand piano, one of the finest January had ever seen.
The music was coming from that piano and it was being
played by Lance.

He sat with his back to her, his fingers picking out
the chords and notes of the Schumann's piece that was
so evocative of playgrounds and bedtime stories and all
childhood's pleasures. With a pang, she remembered her
own father playing that very piece for her when she was
a little girl. It was her father who had given her the gift
of music. She stood perfectly still listening. Tears came
to her eyes as they inevitably did when she was so poign-
antly reminded of her late parent.

"This room is private," Lance said without turning
around. He had stopped playing. She wondered at first
how he had known she was there, then realized there
was a mirror on the back wall and that she was reflected
in it.

"Sorry," she said, "I didn't know." She turned as if
to go, using the opportunity to quickly wipe at her eyes,
hoping he hadn't seen the tears.

"How'd you find it?" Lance said.

She turned around. "It was an accident. I was just
looking for a place to get away from all the noise and
people out there. I found the den off the corridor and
then heard someone playing Schumann and wandered in.
You play awfully well."

"Don't sound so surprised," said Lance sarcastically,
swinging around on the piano bench to face her. "I *am*
a musician, you know."

"I know," January said hastily. Once again they were
getting off on the wrong foot. "It's just that most rock

musicians don't have much classical training."

"Most do," Lance said, correcting her. "They don't advertise it, though, because they think it's bad for the image. How'd you know it was Schumann?"

"'Scenes from Childhood,' one of my favorite pieces. My father used to play it for me when I was a little girl."

Lance said nothing. He was staring at her curiously. "Were you crying?" he asked abruptly.

"Not really."

"Come here," he said. "Sit down." He patted the piano bench. She sat down beside him and he examined her face. "You were crying, weren't you? Why?"

"The music . . . my father . . . he used to play it. He died a few years ago." She took a deep breath, laughed shakily. "You'd think I'd be over it by now."

Lance turned back to the piano keys, let his fingers drift over them, picking out notes at random. "No," he said, "I don't think we ever get over the deaths of those close to us, especially parents. How long were you listening?"

"Only a few minutes."

"Do you live alone?"

"Yes," January said.

"Where?"

"Laurel Canyon. I have a little house. It's not much but I like it."

"What do you do in your spare time?"

January laughed. "Spare time is something I don't have much of. I garden a little. Read. Listen to music."

"What kind of music?"

"Classical, rock, folk, everything. I thought I came out here to interview you."

Lance shrugged. "Why bother? You'll just say what you want anyway."

"Hey," January said, "let's not start that stuff again, okay? I listened to your music and found out you were good. If you had checked my credentials as a reporter, you'd have found I was known for my honesty and fairness."

"In your profession, honesty and fairness don't mean a thing."

"Why do you hate the press so much?"

"I have my reasons. Come on." Lance stood up. "Let's get out of here. If you want an interview, we'll go do an interview."

He was barefoot, in faded jeans and a leather vest without a shirt. His skin was tan and his muscles well defined. Against the warm brown of his face, his green eyes seemed almost turquoise. There was laughter in them as he noticed January staring at him. "Come on." He took her hand. "Get up. You'd think you'd never seen a rock star before. On your feet, woman. We'll see just how honest and fair you are."

She pulled her hand out of his. "Where do you want to go?"

"Your place," he said with a smile. "It sounds nice. I like your hair up." He touched the back of her neck gently. "Did you do that for me? If you can't get a story one way, try another?"

She jerked away from him. "I put it up because it's hot," she said angrily.

He grinned. "My, you're touchy. On second thought I liked it better down. You have beautiful hair." He stepped back and looked at her. "As a matter of fact, you're a beautiful woman. I hadn't noticed."

"Thanks a lot," she said sarcastically.

"For what? Not having noticed? I thought looks weren't important to you liberated, professional women. *Ms*. Warburton," he bowed mockingly. "Come on. Where's your car?"

"Out front," she answered, not at all sure if she wanted Lance Devlin in her house. She wondered why she was going along with this. It had been a long drive out; now he wanted her to turn around and drive them all the way back—and then drive him home again later, she supposed. Oh, the ego of rock stars!

As if reading her mind, he said, "I have to be in Hollywood tonight anyway, at the recording studio.

Someone in the band'll get me home after. Let's go."
He headed for the door then stopped, seeing her hesitation. "You want that interview, don't you?"

She nodded. He led her back through the den, down
the corridor, and into a room she hadn't seen.

"Got to get a shirt," he said.

It was his bedroom, Spartan and simply furnished with
a wide bed, and it had doors leading out to the beach.
The room, done in dark blue and white, had a distinctly
masculine air to it and was very clean. He must have a
maid, January thought.

"You can meet the band tonight," he said, pulling a
silk shirt and a pair of boots out of the closet.

"Tonight?" said January.

"At the recording studio."

"But..."

"If you're going to be traveling with L. A. Expressway,
you might as well start now," he said. He took the vest
off and started to slip on the shirt.

January averted her eyes from his body, wondering
if he intended to change his pants in front of her too.
She fixed her eyes on the ocean beyond the glass doors.

"What's the matter?" he said softly. "Don't like to
watch me changing my clothes? Most women love it."

Before January could come back with any of the fast
retorts that flashed through her mind, the door was flung
open. A girl, her skin golden brown against the pale pink
of an almost invisible bikini, her long hair white-blond,
pranced in. She looked like a model with her incredibly
long legs and slender body.

"Hey, Lance," she said, gliding up to him and putting
her arms around his neck. "When are you coming out?
We need some entertainment."

"Later," he said, giving her a quick kiss on the lips.
"I have business right now."

"What kind of business?"

"Press," he said.

The blonde noticed January for the first time. Her
eyes swept over her coldly and then dismissed her. She

moved closer to Lance. "Can't it wait?"

"Nope," said Lance, disentangling her arms from his neck. "Kim, this is January Warburton, reporter for *Offbeat*. January, Kim Chiles, actress and..."

"And personal groupie to Lance," Kim said challengingly.

January unexpectedly found herself blushing. With all her years around the rock scene, groupies were something she'd never been able to get used to.

"Down, girl," he said, patting Kim and grinning at the sight of January's blush. "This here's a reporter and we wouldn't want you to get a bad rep, now would we?"

"She can call me anything she likes," Kim said easily.

Lance twined his fingers in her hair and tugged it gently. She leaned against him. "Now, now," he said teasingly, "don't get carried away. Come on," he said to January, "let's get going." He kissed Kim lightly and pushed her away from him. "I'll see you later."

"When?" Kim demanded.

"Much later," said Lance. "We're recording tonight."

"I'll come down to the studio," Kim offered.

"No one allowed in the studio," said Lance. "You know the rules."

"But..."

"No buts," Lance said firmly. "Back to the pool with you, girl. Keep that lovely body in shape for me. Ready?" he said to January. Before January could say a word, he was out of the door and striding down the corridor. She hurried after him, sensing but not seeing Kim's angry glance as they left together.

No need to waste your time getting angry with me, January wanted to tell Kim. After her experience with Mike Stone, the last thing she was ever going to let herself do was get involved with a guy in the music business—especially one who went for vapid blondes, as Lance obviously did.

January drove easily. It was a relief to be out of that house, but she felt edgy being alone with Lance. He rolled the window down as they headed out onto the highway, then leaned against the door, one knee propped up against the dashboard, and took a deep breath of air. She kept her eyes on the road but could feel him watching her.

"Pull over there," he said suddenly.

She slowed down for the traffic, then pulled across the highway into the parking lot of the place he pointed to. It was a large roadside nursery filled with plants and flowers.

"Wait here," he said, leaping out of the car and running across the lot. He returned minutes later with two large white azaleas in terra-cotta pots.

"Those are lovely!"

"For a friend," Lance said, setting them down on the back seat of her car.

"Do you plan to take them to the recording studio with you?"

"Nope. I'll deliver them before we go."

January said nothing but had unappealing visions of having to drive him all over the place delivering flowers and whatever else he chose to buy before going to the studio.

"Don't worry," he said, "it's not far out of your way."

January turned to look at him. "You have the most uncanny knack of reading my mind."

"I know," he said with a smile. "It bothers you, doesn't it?"

She shrugged. "A little."

"Don't let it," he said as they continued driving. "It's just a bad habit of mine. You didn't like Kim, did you?"

"She's all right," January said noncommittally, turning left onto Sunset Boulevard.

"Liar," Lance said softly. "You didn't like her. I thought you were known for your honesty."

She said nothing. If Kim was his girlfriend, who was she to judge her?

"January," Lance said thoughtfully, "are you as cold

and wintry as your name?"

"Some people think so," she answered, remembering some of the things Mike had said before she left him. Ice queen, he had called her, simply because after only four months of marriage she found it impossible to accept his having an affair with another woman—no matter how casual he claimed it was.

"I don't think you are," Lance said, tracing a line with one finger from her knee to midway up her thigh.

"Don't," January gasped, pushing his hand away.

"I think you're very warm-blooded," he said. "Just shy. Why are you so shy of men, January?"

"I'm not," she said. There was no way she was going to discuss her personal life with him. But he was right, she was shy with men, and had been since leaving Mike. She had been more disillusioned than she had thought possible, and she wasn't rushing into a relationship with anyone after that experience.

"Yes you are," he said. "You jump when I touch you. You blush if I even look at you. Why?"

"It's really none of your business," she snapped.

"Ah," Lance said, "I see. I am meant to reveal all the secrets of my heart to you in an interview, bare my soul as it were, and you don't have to give a thing in return. Is that the way it works?"

She bit her lip. He had a point. "I was married," she said shortly. "To a music producer. Mike Stone, you've probably heard of him. He...he succumbed to a little platinum-haired groupie four months after we got married. Satisfied?"

Lance grinned. "And all people in the music business are the same, right? Unfaithful, unpredictable, and unreliable, ready to run off with the first bleached blonde that comes their way."

January had to laugh, he'd nailed her feelings so exactly. "That's just about it," she said.

His hand returned to her thigh. "And what if I said I was different?"

She pushed his hand away again. "I wouldn't believe you for a second."

Lance laughed. "When you decide to get honest, you sure are honest, aren't you?"

"Absolutely," she said flatly.

"So how long's it been since you had a man?"

"That really is none of your business," said January.

"That long?" said Lance. "We really ought to do something about that," he said with a teasing smile.

January was turning the car up Laurel Canyon Boulevard as he said it and caught a glimpse of his face. "Lance Devlin," she said, "I'm warning you. Don't you try anything with me. I took two years of karate and I promise you, I'll send you flying across the room in two seconds."

"Thanks for the warning," he said, as if he didn't take her seriously at all. "No wonder your body's in such great shape. That pretty little dress doesn't hide a thing, you know."

"You're impossible," she said as she turned the car down the little dirt road that led to her house.

"One-track mind," Lance retorted as she parked the car and they got out. "That's what they all tell me."

"I bet they *all* do," she muttered, grabbing her bag and unlocking the door to the house, wondering for the thousandth time what on earth she was doing bringing him here.

"This is nice," Lance said, looking at the beds of daisies, nasturtiums, petunias, and geraniums. "Just as I imagined."

She started to go inside.

"Wait," he said, "you forgot something."

"I did?"

He went to her car and drew out the two potted azaleas. "I had a feeling they'd look nice on either side of your front door. He set them down on the stoop. "And they do."

"For me?" she said with surprise.

"For you," he said.

For the second time that day, tears came to her eyes. "But why?"

He shrugged. "Maybe because it's so easy to make you cry."

"Oh, damn you," she said going into the house, and then turned quickly to thank him, feeling she'd been rude and unappreciative. He was right behind her, and before she could even get the words "Thank you" out of her mouth, he'd caught her face in his hands and was kissing her. His lips were amazingly gentle against hers, and she felt a sudden dizziness rush through her that she'd never felt before, not even when Mike had kissed her. She wanted to break away from him but instead felt her body melting against his.

"Very warm-blooded," he murmured, drawing back from her. He kissed her again lightly, on either cheek. "Come on, we have an interview to do."

Flushed and embarrassed by her response, January led him into the house.

The house was wood, all pine and cedar inside with wide floor boards, a beamed ceiling, plants hanging from hooks and tucked on shelves between books. There was a rocking chair by the paned window, a hooked rug on the floor, and a window seat filled with embroidered pillows. On the back of the sofa was an antique patchwork quilt that January had found at a garage sale and bargained down to practically nothing.

"Homey," said Lance, settling down on the sofa. "I like it here. Okay, boss, fire away. Hit me with all the questions you like."

"Do you always go around kissing reporters?" January blurted without thinking.

Lance laughed. "Only ones who look like they need it."

"I look like I *need* kissing, do I?" January said.

"Young lady," he replied, "this is no way to conduct an interview. You are meant to ask me where I grew up, what's my favorite color, how I like my steaks cooked. . . .

Don't tell me I have to teach you your job."

"Oh shut up," she said. She got out her tape recorder and notebook.

"Let's skip the interview," said Lance. "You'll learn everything you need to know about me on the road."

"I can't." She sighed. This just might prove to be the most difficult assignment she'd ever undertaken. "I have to write something."

"Write about the recording studio. I'll give you an exclusive. We've never let anyone in the recording studio before. Afterwards, I'll take you out to dinner and answer any questions you have."

Getting into the studio with the band as they put the finishing touches on their new album would make an ideal story. "And what'll we do now?" January asked.

"I know one thing we could do," Lance said, looking first at her and then at her bedroom door with a teasing grin.

"Forget it," said January firmly. She grinned back at him. "But I know what we *will* do. Take off your shirt."

"What?"

"Go on," she said, "take it off. Or are you shy with women all of a sudden?"

Watching her questioningly, he unbuttoned his shirt and took it off. "Now what?"

"Now follow me," she said. She led him out to the garden. "Hope you don't mind getting your jeans dirty." She handed him a spade. "You do know the difference between a weed and a flower, don't you?"

"I can manage," Lance said, an utterly baffled expression on his face.

"Good," said January. "Get to work."

"Where are you going?" he asked as she headed back to the house.

"To slip into something more comfortable," she said with a teasing smile.

She came out a few minutes later in a pair of cut-off denims and an old T-shirt.

Side by side on their hands and knees, they thinned

geraniums and yanked weeds.

"I used to do this with my mother when I was a kid," Lance said. "We had a house in the Valley before we moved to Malibu."

"You mean that house is your parents' house?"

He stopped and gave her a sharp look. "It was. My parents are dead."

"I'm sorry," she murmured, remembering her own tears for her father earlier that day.

"My mother was a concert pianist," said Lance. "She said gardening was good for the hands."

"And your father?" January asked softly.

"Violinist. Whole family of musicians. I grew up in it. I learned to play those pieces by Schumann when I was six. My mother taught me."

"What happened to them? Your parents?"

"Plane crash, flying back from a concert in Budapest twelve years ago. I'm surprised you didn't hear of it. They were pretty famous."

"Devlin?" January shook her head. "I don't remember..."

"Not Devlin. That was my mother's maiden name. I took it when I decided to go professional. I didn't want to get jobs because of my name."

"Then what were their names?"

Lance looked at her strangely. "You didn't do your homework at all, did you? Some reporter you are. The information is available, you know."

The sun was warm on January's back. She didn't feel like arguing or defending herself. She was too comfortable.

As if Lance understood and felt the same way, he didn't push the issue, but said simply, "Braun, Franz and Lenora Braun were my parents."

"I remember them," January exclaimed. "I saw them in concert as a child, often. My parents used to take me. No wonder," she breathed softly.

"No wonder what?"

"You're such a good musician and composer. With

a background like that..."

"Thank you, madame," he said.

"Is it private information?" she said. "I mean do you want it off the record? Because if you do, I'll respect that. I'll see that it doesn't get printed."

"I'd appreciate that," he replied.

"You got it," January said. "No problem." Even as she made the promise, something nagged at her, some story from her childhood or early teens that she'd heard about the Brauns, specifically Lenora Braun, who had been an extraordinarily beautiful woman. Blonde, vibrant, regal, she had been queen of European and American concert halls. And them something had happened. But what? Some scandal. January's intuition told her it was better not to ask Lance. She'd find out on Monday when she got into the office and did a little research.

He saw her frown. "What is it?" he asked.

"Huh? Oh, nothing. Just wondering if we should water now or later."

Lance glanced up at the sky. The sun was beginning to go down. "Might as well do it now," he said. "Sun's low enough."

She went to get the hose. "Want a beer?" she asked when she came back, hose turned on. "It's hot, isn't it?" she said, wiping the perspiration off her forehead.

"I'd love one," Lance said. "Here, give me that. I'll water while you get the beers."

She came out minutes later, two open cans in her hands. A mischievous gleam came into Lance's eye as she approached. Before she knew what was happening, he had turned the hose full on her. "Damn," she said, trying to avoid the cooling spray. "Lance, stop it!"

She set the cans down on the stoop, ducked out of his way, and raced to the corner of the house to where the hose was connected. He ran after her, still dousing her. By the time she got the faucet turned off, her clothes were soaked, her hair drenched. Lance was laughing uproariously, like a kid.

Seeing his face, January was unable to get mad. She

stood there, water running down her body, shaking her head, staring at him. "I don't believe you did this to me."

He wasn't laughing anymore. "I don't believe how good you look soaking wet."

She looked down at herself. Her T-shirt was clinging to her skin, her breasts outlined in sharp relief, her nipples hard against the thin material. She didn't move as Lance walked toward her and putting his hands on her shoulders, began to kiss her. Instead of pushing him away, her arms went around him, pulling herself closer against him, the warmth of his bare chest penetrating the wet T-shirt. His mouth against hers seemed to take possession of her whole being, and she wanted nothing but to be in the arms of this man. He kissed her cheeks, her eyelids, the side of her neck, and whispered in her ear, as his arms tightened around her. "You are so beautiful, January." Even as he said it, a picture flashed in her mind of Kim: her long silver hair, her sleek model's body; Lance's arms around her, Lance whispering in her ear. Furiously January broke free of him.

"Leave me alone, Lance Devlin," she said, ignoring the fact that she was breathing too quickly and that her nipples were even harder than before. "Don't touch me. Just keep your dirty hands off me."

There was a mocking light in his eyes as he held up his hands. "Dirt from your garden only, my dear," he said.

She pretended not to hear him as she stormed into the house, marched into the bathroom, locked the door, stripped off her wet clothes, and got into the shower. But once under the hot water, she found herself leaning against the wall realizing weakly just how much she'd wanted Lance. It was sex only, she thought to herself as she soaped her body; sex for him, sex for her. She wouldn't give in to it. Not this time. She'd mistaken sex for love once before and she'd never do that again. And yet as she ran the soapy washcloth over her flat stomach and high breasts, she found herself wondering what Lance's hands would feel like on her body.

She got out of the shower and went into her bedroom wrapped in a terry towel robe. She half expected to find that Lance had called a cab and left. She was startled to find him instead lying on her bed, fully dressed, thumbing through a magazine. Before she could say a word, he stood up.

"Don't worry, January. I'm not going to touch you. You want me as much as I want you, and you know it. When you're ready, just tell me." He went out to the living room. "Hurry up and get changed," he called to her. "I've got to be over at the recording studio in half an hour."

"You sound like my ex-husband," she called out to him angrily.

She heard him laugh in response and sat down hard on her bed, head in her hands. She had never felt so confused.

Twenty-four hours ago, her life had been predictable. Now she felt turned upside down and inside out. One half of her wanted to throw Lance out of the house, tell Adrian to get someone else for the job, and never see Lance Devlin again. The other half of her wanted to go out to the living room just as she was, in her long white robe, settle down on the couch with him, and simply give herself to him completely.

The most terrible part was that she had the distinct impression Lance knew exactly what she was feeling.

chapter

3

JANUARY tucked the white T-shirt into her designer jeans, then slipped into a soft loose white linen jacket. Ready, she thought, running a brush through her dark hair, slightly damp from the shower. She checked the contents of her bag to make sure everything was there: camera, notebook, pens. While dressing she'd made up her mind to announce to Lance that from now on their relationship was strictly business. She squared her shoulders and walked out to the living room.

"Hi," Lance said. "You look great. This is Rick, my road manager and, when I'm not on the road, my driver."

The blond young man who was sprawled comfortably on January's favorite armchair grinned up at her and took another swallow of beer. "Glad to meet you," he said affably.

"How did you get here?" January started to ask, but Lance interrupted her before she could finish the sentence.

"I called him. I thought you'd done enough driving for one day. Come on, the car's out front."

"You were out at Lance's earlier today, weren't you?" Rick asked.

January nodded, slightly numb. Lance's effrontery amazed her—that he would simply use her phone, call up some stranger, ask him over without a word to her. She cautioned herself that she was overreacting. After all Rick was Lance's road manager and driver. She vaguely remembered seeing him on the floor drinking beer—he'd offered her some. As he eased himself out of her chair and ambled to her door, she wondered if he was like most road managers she'd known. Usually they were pushy, egotistical semialcoholics guarding their rock stars with incredible tenacity, keeping the press away, and letting the girls in. In his faded jeans, red satin jacket, hair below his collar, and with beer in hand, Rick fit the image.

"We were in grade school together," said Lance, once again seeming to read her mind. "He's one of my best friends. He takes care of everything for me."

I bet he does, January thought cynically.

Taking up most of the small dirt driveway was a black limousine, sparkling clean, smoked-glass windows preventing anyone from seeing inside. January had to laugh at the incongruity of Rick in his old jeans and satin jacket driving a car like this. "Not exactly your typical chauffeur's uniform," she commented.

"Yeah," Rick said easily, opening the car doors and sliding into the front.

Lance helped January into the back. "He likes being alone up there. He has his own tape deck in the front; we have ours here."

It wasn't the first limo January had been in, but she was always impressed by the spaciousness. She stretched her legs out comfortably.

"I'd offer you some champagne," Lance said, "but I don't drink before a studio session. Impairs the work."

He clicked a cassette into the recorder in the back of the limo. January was surprised to hear soft strains of classical music instead of the usual rock. It was a Mozart concerto.

"That's my father on violin, my mother on piano," said Lance. Before January knew what was happening, Lance had taken her hand in his.

"Lance," she started to say, but he put a finger to her lips.

"Ssh," he said. "Listen."

Gently he caressed the palm of her hand with his thumb. She felt a melting sensation inside her stomach and stole a glance at his profile. He was intent on the music, his eyes half-closed, his lips slightly parted. "The music keeps them alive for me," he said suddenly, turning to look at her. "Do you know what I mean?"

She nodded. She knew exactly what he meant.

"I thought you'd understand," he said, turning toward her.

She realized he was going to kiss her. She pulled her hand out of his. "Lance, please, don't. Look, we've got to . . . this has to be . . ."

"Business only?" he said in a mocking voice, making her feel like a fool.

"Yes," she said with all the strength she could summon, "business only."

"Okay," he said, "have it your way." He withdrew from her. There was a strained silence between them, an awkward tension.

"Lance," she said "couldn't we just be friends?"

"No," he said, facing her, eyes blazing, "we couldn't. You know it and I know it. You want me and I want you. How long will you deny it?"

She ran a nervous hand through her hair. "We've only known each other two days."

"What does it take? A lifetime? You're a reporter, aren't you? Your job is to have precise instincts and perceptions. Don't you trust them?"

"I don't trust you," she blurted out.

"Don't you? Or is it yourself you don't trust? Burned once and afraid to fall in love again. Is that the way it goes?"

His assessment was too accurate for January's comfort. "Who said anything about falling in love?" she murmured.

Lance just looked at her. Under the spell of his green eyes, she found herself blushing crimson. He grinned. "No one," he said. "I'm just a typical rock-and-roller. All I want is your body." He laughed lightly.

January turned away. She wished she could believe he was telling the truth, that he wanted to go to bed with her and that was all. But something in his eyes made her unsure. And if only, she thought, he didn't arouse those sensual feelings in her, feelings that had lain dormant for so long.

The limo pulled up in front of the old art deco building on Hollywood Boulevard that housed Platinum's recording studios. Rick switched off the ignition, jumped out, and opened the doors for them.

"Come on in and meet the band," said Lance coolly, as if nothing had taken place between them.

Samson, the drummer, brown hair cut short to accommodate the New Wave look, resembled a small, powerful bulldog. Few people realized the incredible strength it took to play the drums night after night, but in Samson's build one could see it. Derek, the bass player, had the solemn, almost intellectual look January associated with many bass players she'd known. He shook her hand gravely, saying what a pleasure it was going to be to have such an attractive woman on the road with them.

"Bored with me, are you?" Teri said with a grin. "Hi, January," she said, "I can't tell you what a relief it's going to be having another woman along. All these guys get tiring after a while—they're all yours. Except this one, my husband, Joel. He's the piano player, and he's taken."

Joel, bearded and teddy-bearish looking, smiled. "I can see why Lance broke one of his cardinal rules. For you, I'd even consider breaking a few rules myself."

Teri gave him a friendly kick. "Just try it," she said.

"What rule is that?" January asked, adding quickly, "I mean, that Lance broke."

"No press," Samson said. "Didn't you know? He's notorious for never even giving an interview."

"Okay," Lance interrupted. "Introductions are over. Let's get to work."

"He's also a slavedriver," Teri said. "And a perfectionist. You're not going to believe what goes in that studio."

"If we sit out here gabbing all night, nothing'll go on," said Lance.

Teri saluted cheerfully. "Yes, boss. See you later," she said to January.

The musicians filed into the studio. They were nice, January thought. Being on the road with them was going to be fun.

"You can sit in here," Lance said, indicating the sound booth where the engineers and producer were. He paused before entering the studio. "How about dinner later? After the session. Business only," he said with a mocking grin. "You can ask questions then. Maybe I'll even answer them."

He was standing close to her, only inches away from her body. January realized with a shock that he didn't even need to touch her for her to respond to him. All it took was his physical nearness. "Yes," she murmured, "dinner would be nice."

He smiled, reached up, brushed a strand of hair away from her face, and then turned and went into the studio. Once again she had the uncomfortable sensation that he knew exactly what she was feeling.

The sound engineer pulled up a chair for her. Through

the window that faced into the studio she could see the musicians taking their places, tuning their instruments, adjusting their headphones. Lance gave a signal to the engineer, who turned knobs and shifted levers on the large console in front of him, talking to the band through the headset he wore. Lance and Teri stepped up to their mikes. The song opened with Joel on piano, then the others came in: Lance on lead guitar picking up the melody; Samson on drums setting the tempo.

Rick leaned against the back wall of the sound booth, toothpick between his teeth, watching. Their producer, Jay Livingston, was one of Platinum's best. He was a close friend of Adrian's and knew January and *Offbeat Magazine* well. It was he who had convinced Lance that he ought to start cooperating with the press and then had set the wheels in motion with Adrian. He came over and sat down beside January. He was a gray-haired man who'd been around the music business a long time. He had also, January recalled bitterly, known her ex-husband, Mike Stone.

"Got a moment?" Jay whispered.

January nodded and they stepped outside into the thickly carpeted, totally soundproofed corridor.

"How are you getting along with Lance?" Jay asked.

January shrugged.

"Don't let him get on your nerves. He has bad feelings about the press."

"So I've noticed."

"Well, he's got good reason. He'll tell you about it if you want. Anyway, it's all on record. You can look it up. The fact that he invited you down here tonight is a good sign. He must like you."

January felt her cheeks flush slightly and hoped Jay wouldn't notice.

"They're good musicians and good people. Being on the road with them should be easy. I think we've got a hit album on our hands with this one, and a hit group. Boston and New York will tell. They're the big places." Jay smiled. "I can't ask you to write all favorable stories, but anything you can do for them, I'd appreciate."

"I like their music," January said simply. "They're good. Lance is terrific."

"He's also a good man," Jay said. "Loyal, faithful, one of the best in the business. There aren't many like him. His band loves him."

So do his groupies, January thought, but said nothing.

"They're laying down the last two tracks tonight. Lance had recorded them once, but he wasn't satisfied with the quality."

"Teri said he's a perfectionist."

"He is," Jay answered as they went back into the sound booth to listen.

They ran through one song three times before Lance was satisfied. Then they all gathered in the sound booth to listen to it. Everyone liked it. On a table were an urn of coffee, fresh fruit juices, Coca Cola, and beer. The band helped themselves to what they wanted as they listened. January noticed that Lance drank only fruit juice. She had also noticed that as L. A. Expressway played, they put as much heart and soul into recording in the studio as she imagined they must before a live audience of thousands. She knew it was that drive, that all-out effort, that was catapulting them to success. In music, as in anything, it was giving everything that counted.

Teri wandered over to January, Coke in hand. Her long shag haircut was wildly disheveled from the abandoned movement that accompanied her singing. Her face glowed softly, glistening with perspiration. January had liked her immediately. Her open, friendly smile and wide blue eyes put one at ease. January felt certain that in Teri she had at least one friend in the group.

Lance was leaning over the sound console, talking with the engineer. Teri glanced over at him and then said quietly to January, "He really likes you."

January was startled. "Who?"

"Lance, dopey," Teri said with a grin. "I don't know how you've done it, being press and all, but I think he has a genuine crush on you."

January blushed. "Well..."

"So it's mutual," Teri said. "I can see this is going to be a hot tour."

"Business only," January said. "We already agreed to that." As she said it, she looked over at Lance to see his eyes on her. There was something unfathomable in his expression.

Teri saw it too. "Business only," she said. "Good luck. When Lance wants something, he goes for it. And he wants you. Any fool can see that. He can't take his eyes off of you. You should have seen him when you walked out with Jay. I could swear," she said with an imitation Texas accent, "that man was just green with jealousy." She chuckled and shook her head. "Poor Derek."

"What do you mean?" January asked.

"Didn't you notice? He developed instant infatuation with one look at you. Oops, the boss is signaling. Back to work."

Teri followed the rest of the band back into the studio.

They may all be developing crushes and infatuations, thought January, but they sure aren't showing it. She was surprised to find herself hurt that during their break Lance had neither come up to her once nor spoken to her. Except for that one moment when she'd seen him watching her, he seemed to be ignoring her as if she weren't even there.

It only took them one run-through to get the second song down exactly as Lance wanted it. At the end, the band looked tired but exhilarated. Jay came up to January.

"Lance has agreed that it's okay for you to take some pictures of the band in the studio if you like."

"Great," January said, who had already been planning the story she was going to write.

She grabbed her camera, took a series of shots of them, asking them to play a song through so the poses would be natural and real.

"Anything in particular you'd like to hear?" Lance asked. "You did say you'd listened to the tapes, didn't you?" He grinned.

Despite herself, January grinned back, remembering their first meeting. "Yes," she said, "play 'Diamonds of the Sea.' It's my favorite."

"'Diamonds' it is," said Lance.

He sang it beautifully, even better than on the tape. The whole band seemed to be playing the song just for her. And as she took her pictures, January felt united with them. They were working together, giving to her and the camera. And she was working for and with them, going for the shots that would portray the feeling and flavor of L.A. Expressway the best. The final pictures she took were of Lance, and as his face came into focus through the viewfinder, his eyes seemed to be directly on her, his voice caressing the words especially for her. She was mesmerized. Her finger pushed the camera's lever automatically. She was riveted to him. He might have been playing a guitar and she taking photos but it felt as though they were touching. As his voice hit the last note, she felt a sort of sigh go through her, and then the song was over, the spell broken. There was a moment of silence and then the band began to laugh and congratulate one another, setting down their instruments.

"That was great," Derek said, coming up to January shyly. "I hate having my picture taken, but you made me feel really comfortable."

"If she got some good enough photos, maybe we can use them on the album cover," Joel added. "The ones we have stink. I've seen your work in the past. You're good. We're lucky to have you going on the road with us."

January said nothing. She felt Lance's eyes on her. He was still holding his guitar, watching her.

"Thank you," she said, going over to him, "for the song."

"My pleasure," he said. "Ready for dinner?"

She nodded.

"By the way, Joel's right. We don't have decent pictures. Maybe you could come up with an album cover for us."

"I'd love to try."

Lance nodded.

So it was back to business again, thought January. She was beginning to wish she'd kept her mouth shut.

"We hit the road Thursday," Lance called out to the group. "Get a lot of rest. It's a short tour, but it's an important one. We've never played the east before and we've got to make them love us. So take it easy for the next four days, and be ready. We fly out of Los Angeles at ten A.M., Thursday morning, and get into Washington, D.C. sometime in the afternoon. If anyone needs a ride to the airport, call Rick. And remember, he must have all your equipment by four o'clock Wednesday afternoon." Lance turned to January. "Okay, Ms. Reporter, dinnertime."

Over sushi and sake in one of L.A.'s best Japanese restaurants, Lance told January more about the band. Most of them he'd known all his life. He and Teri had gone to kindergarten together. Samson was the only newcomer. It had taken them awhile to find the drummer who was just right for them. "We've paid our dues," Lance said. "We've been playing in garages and basements since we were teenagers. This is actually the third album we've cut. Thanks to lousy promotion, the other two disappeared practically before they were released."

"Lousy promotion," January chided gently, "or your lousy attitude toward the press?"

Lance shrugged and refilled their small porcelain cups with more hot wine. "Both, probably."

January smiled. The sake seemed to warm her whole body, making it tingle. She leaned back in the duskily lit leather booth. "That recording session was great. I really enjoyed it. The band's good."

"One of the best," grinned Lance.

"You're not modest at all, are you?"

"Nope. How about some green tea ice cream? It's delicious here."

"I can't. I'm too full." January patted her stomach.

"You look fine to me," Lance said.

"Don't start," January said warningly but with a smile.

"Yes ma'am," he said. "Home then?"

"Home," January said.

"Your place or mine?" Clearly he was teasing her.

"If that sake hadn't made me feel so good," January said, "I'd kick you."

"Come on." Lance slid out of the booth and took her hand.

Rick was waiting out front for them with the limo. Lance hadn't let go of January's hand when he'd helped her out of the booth and was still holding it as Rick opened the car door for them. For some reason she found herself not bothering to pull it away. The wine, she decided as she got into the car.

The window between the front and the back was closed. The back of the limo was softly lit, the front dark as Rick started driving. Lance opened the window to the front, said something to Rick, then reshut it.

"Where are we going?" January asked as they drove up Laurel Canyon Boulevard right past the little street where they should have turned off to her house.

"A drive," he answered. "I like to see the city at night."

Before she could say a word, Lance had twisted in the seat, gathering her into his arms as he did so, so that their bodies were stretched lengthwise, Lance's back against the side of the car, his body supporting hers.

"Lance," she protested weakly.

"Don't worry," he said. "I just want to hold you."

His arms drew her closer. She felt the rise and fall of his chest against her body and relaxed into it, her breathing seeming to fall into rhythm with his. With one hand he brushed her heavy fall of hair off her neck, gently kissing her just above the shoulder.

She moaned softly. Feeling she no longer had any control of her body, she turned even more toward him so that she was pressed against him. She lifted her face. His kisses at first were gentle, then more insistent. She couldn't resist them, returned them equally insistently, her arms going around his neck. His body shifted. She felt the lean hardness of his thighs against hers. His fingers traced patterns over her, sliding the linen jacket off her shoulders, moving down the bare skin of her arms, across her back, under the thin cotton of her T-shirt. His hands were moving up over her ribs to the soft underpart of her breasts and she was arching to meet his touch, when he pushed her back from him to look at her face.

"Business only?" he asked with a mocking smile that she could just see in the dim light. "Is that still the way you want it?"

Her whole body was aching for him, trembling from his touch, but the anger that rose, at him, at herself, extinguished the heat she felt. Abruptly she was aware of Rick in the front seat driving, obviously knowing everything they were doing. Aware also of the way she felt he'd tricked her—the hot wine, the ride up into the Hollywood hills, where the air was cool, filled with the pungent fragrance of sage.

She muttered his name, then pulled sharply away. "How could you?" She tugged at her shirt and ran her fingers through her tangled hair. She felt a rush of mortification. How easily he'd made them comfortable on this back seat, how many times he must have seduced women here. And she thought, with added bitterness, how many little groupies had probably given themselves to him here!

"Take me home," she said, her jaw tight.

Lance's eyes were narrow as he watched her. "No problem," he said in a tight, cold voice. He rapped on the window and it slid open a few inches. He gave Rick January's address.

"He knows where it is," she said tautly. "After all, he's been there before."

The ride home seemed very quick. In seconds, it seemed, they were at January's door. She let herself out of the car, realizing even as she did so, things were turning into a hopeless mess. Well, it was Lance's fault, she told herself. If he'd just leave her alone.... But he wouldn't. As she walked to her door and turned the key in the lock, she realized he was right behind her.

He grabbed her by the wrist as she started to go in, spinning her around to face him. "I'm not going to apologize. It's your fault. You're a little tease, one moment coming on to me, the next withdrawing."

January's mouth dropped open. "I don't know what you're talking about."

"Oh yes you do. You didn't resist me in the car. Not until I said something. And you didn't take your hand out of mine when I took it earlier. What you can't do is take any responsibility for your own desire. You want to be swept along and then the next day get mad at me and say it's my fault. Well I'm not playing your games, January. Sooner or later you're going to admit to wanting me."

"Fine," she snapped. "I do want you. So what? So do Kim and Susie and Becky and all your other little groupies, whatever their names are. But I'm not one of them and don't get it into your head that I am. Yes, you're hard to resist. Yes, I'm attracted to you. Yes, I'd probably even like to go to bed with you. But, guess what? I'm not going to do it. I have no intention of being one more on your string of women. I wouldn't lower myself. So just go on home to Kim or whoever is waiting for you. I'm sure there are at least half a dozen."

To her astonishment, as her anger abated, she saw Lance was laughing. "Kim," he said. "Oh my poor deluded January." He reached for her, but she twisted away. He threw his hands up in the air. "Okay, have it your way, my sweet. Kim," he shook his head, laughing harder. "When you really want to know about me and Kim, ask Teri or someone in the band. I know you won't listen to me. Sweet dreams," he said, stepping down from her doorstep and walking to the car. "Do you need a ride to the airport on Thursday?"

January shook her head, and watched, dazed, as the limo drove off.

She couldn't go on the tour, she thought as she got ready for bed. She just couldn't. Adrian would have to find someone else to replace her. But as she slid down between the sheets in the cool darkness, she found herself remembering Lance's hands and mouth on her body, wanting them again, wishing he were here in bed beside her. Outside her window crickets chirped. Somehow she slept.

chapter

4

ON SUNDAY afternoon, the Sunset office building was empty. The security guard, recognizing January, had opened the door for her, and with her own key she'd let herself into her office. She sat, feet propped on her desk, studying the proof sheet of the photos she'd taken of Lance and L.A. Expressway. They were good. She'd developed them herself in the magazine's darkroom and she was pleased with her work. With a red grease pencil she marked off six, three for her article, three to give to the band. She'd have the prints made of them tomorrow.

One print she'd already made. She picked it up and looked at it. She'd known as soon as she'd seen it on the proof sheet that it would make a great picture. And it did. Lance's eyes stared out with extraordinary intensity; his mouth curved into a half smile. Light played across his hair and the angles of his face. There was a grainy quality to the black-and-white photo, coarse, yet subtle and delicate; like Lance himself, she thought. She knew it was one of the best photographs she'd ever taken. Thoughtfully she slipped it into her desk drawer, questioning herself as she did so. Why, January wondered, was she keeping a picture of Lance for herself? She might kid herself that it was because it was a great shot, but there was more to it than that and she knew it.

She stood up restlessly. A decision had to be made. Tomorrow she had to make up her mind whether she was going on tour or not. If not, she would need to find someone to replace her. An uneasy night's sleep and a busy morning had not brought her any closer to deciding.

Perhaps Lance was right. Perhaps last night had been partly her fault. She should have taken her hand out of his, should have resisted his advances in the car. She paced her office floor. The fact was, January knew, she hadn't wanted to resist him. She had wanted his touch, the feel of his body, his kisses. Even remembering them the next day, a hot wave swept over her body. Well, she couldn't let it happen again. That was all there was to it. But could she prevent it? On tour together, in the close quarters of a bus, no matter how well outfitted, they would be in constant contact with each other. It was true that she wanted him; it was also true that she had no intention of being one more of his string of women.

She sat down again, swinging her chair around to face out the window. There was something else Lance had said—that she was afraid of falling in love again . . .

"Hey, there. It's Sunday. What are you doing here?"

Startled, January swiveled her chair to face the door and Steve Creighton. "I might ask the same of you."

"I came to pick up some papers I left. What are these?" He picked up the proof sheets off her desk, studied them. "Great shots. When'd you take them?"

"Last night, at the recording studio."

Steve raised his eyebrows. "You got into the recording studio? How on earth did you do that?"

January laughed at his incredulous stare. "You always underestimate my abilities."

Wishing Steve would go away, January reminded herself that they had to work together. She knew too well Steve's version of working with people: picking their brains and stealing their notes. She could never understand why Adrian had made him associate editor. Admittedly his organizational skills were exceptional and his sense of design and layout excellent, but Steve had a knack for making anything he wrote sound slightly sordid. He was exploitative, January thought, something no good journalist could afford to be. One of these days he was going to get himself, and the magazine, into serious trouble.

"What do you know about that?" she asked him. "Lance's hatred of the press, I mean."

Steve shrugged. "Not much. I thought maybe you'd find something when you do the research for the profile piece."

"Hey," January said. "I'm doing the interview and pre-tour story as well as going on the road. The profile piece is yours."

"Yeah, well," Steve replied, "I've got all the galleys to go over, the whole paper to proof." He stopped, seeing January's angry stare. "Okay, okay. How about you dig up what info you can in the files? I'll take it from there. Turn your notes into a story."

January sighed but agreed. In some ways she preferred that arrangement. For her own satisfaction, she'd do the research anyway, as Steve well knew. She never trusted anyone to be as thorough as she insisted on being.

"So how do you like Lance?" Steve said with a grin. "I hear he's pretty sexy. You could have a hot time on the road."

January looked at him disdainfully. "It's strictly business," she said. "Not all of us live in the gutter."

Steve laughed. "No one suggested you do it in the gutter—beds are much more comfortable."

January was seething and Steve knew it. He seemed

to enjoy her anger and was still chuckling as he went to the door.

"Gotta go," he said. "Have fun researching. Come up with something good for me, something meaty that I can really sink my teeth into. Nice and juicy for the readers."

"You mean slimy?" January retorted. "That's your style, not mine."

Steve grinned. "Sells papers, and that's our business."

Adrian ought to get rid of him, January thought as Steve disappeared down the hallway. She went over her preliminary notes on Lance and then headed down the corridor to the file room. She would start where she always started when researching a person—at the beginning, with the parents. In Lance's case she was especially interested in his background. Perhaps it would offer some clue as to why he was so hostile to the press. She consulted her notes. His parents had been musicians. She began to thumb through the "B" file.

Braun. She found the file. There was a whole folder on Lenora and Franz Braun, thick with clippings and articles. She carried it back to her desk, sat down, and began to read through it systematically and methodically.

Franz and Lenora had been world-renowned musicians. Lenora especially had received attention, not only for piano playing, but for her magnificent looks and extraordinary stage presence. The press had loved them; and then, according to the articles, Lenora had had an affair. She had become involved with a conductor, a handsome European with dark wavy hair. The scandal became as famous as Lenora herself. After that, for two years she and her husband disappeared from view. There were rumors of divorce, that she had run off with the conductor or someone else, every sort of story the papers could come up with. But the outcome was that no one knew where she was, what she was doing. And then, after two years, Lenora and Franz resurfaced. They announced they would be playing again, giving concerts, just the two of them. They were on their way home from an extraordinarily successful tour of Central Europe when their plane crashed and they were killed.

January, as she read, automatically jotted down the salient facts on a yellow legal pad. Calculating rapidly, she figured Lance must have been about fifteen when the affair took place, seventeen when his parents were killed. Quite a bit younger than she'd been when her father died. A pang of compassion ran through her. Still, it didn't explain his hostility to the press. Certainly it must have been unpleasant seeing the story of his mother's affair plastered everywhere, but the news people were only doing their job. A woman as famous as Lenora Braun must expect to be talked about. It struck January as curious that Lance's mother had continually denied the story. If everyone so obviously knew, it would have been wiser to have simply admitted to it. Despite the talk of divorce, Franz Braun evidently stood by his wife. And it seemed that no one was able to get any statement from the conductor.

January sat back in her chair and stretched. Reason enough for Lance's hostility, she thought, and yet not reason enough. Was there something she had missed? She went through the folder one more time, then went back to the files and pulled out what they had on Lance. She could find nothing to shed any further light on the story. Perhaps, she ruminated, Lance somehow associated his parents' death with the press reports. When her father died, she had learned that grief made the imagination play strange tricks. She had successively blamed herself, her mother, and the entire twentieth century until she gradually was able to accept that his heart condition and the heart attack that had killed him were nobody's fault. If Lance were carrying a twelve-year grudge, it seemed both a shame and a ridiculous waste of energy. Well, through her, maybe he'd learn to be a little more trusting.

And then she smiled to herself. One minute she had been determined not to go on the tour. Now she was not only going, she was intending to change Lance's life.

She picked up one of the clippings and studied again

a childhood photo of Lance. He was seven, hair then very blond, and bright little eyes shining. Without thinking what she was doing, January picked up her scissors and in quick, clean snips cut out the picture. She clipped it to the large photo in her desk. Returning the folders to their files and leaving the photos to be printed in a tray by the darkroom she prepared to leave.

She knew in advance tomorrow was going to be a long day at the office. In twenty-four hours, she had to write a cover story for a magazine that had officially gone to press, which meant that space was limited down to the letter. Not only that, but knowing Steve, she'd probably have to write his story too. The typesetters would go crazy if they didn't have everything by noon on Monday.

Sunday night she spent at home writing. She was back in the office early Monday morning. By eleven-thirty, she had a story she liked. It chronicled the career and life of the band, focusing on Lance but making it clear that these were a group of top professional musicians, most of whom had known each other since childhood. Lance had said the lack of success of their first two albums was in no way due to the quality of the music but to poor promotion. A little research had shown this to be correct, and further research made it evident that to afficionados those two Expressway albums were collectors' items.

Included with the articles she put together were early photos of the band, plus the photos she had taken in the recording studio, and a description of them laying down the last two tracks for their album—an album that January confidently predicted would be number one on the charts. There was no mention of Franz and Lenora Braun. In keeping with past articles, January kept Lance something of a mystery man, a reportorial trick guaranteed to ignite curiosity. Audiences, she had found, loved enigmas.

She reread the article one more time and left it on Steve's desk.

During her lunch break, she took an hour to herself to drive over to Beverly Hills and buy a well-cut khaki jumpsuit made of soft cotton. Bus traveling demanded comfortable clothes. It did not demand the gauzy black dress with the low back and the skirt cut on a bias that she found both irresistible and over her budget. She bought it anyway, and a pair of low-heeled gold sandals—just in case she had reason to dress up, she told herself.

Steve stopped by her office when she got back. "I liked your story," he said. "It's gone to the printers. We're running it exactly the way it is. What kind of background stuff did you dig up on Lance? Anything on his family?"

"Nothing that can be used," January said shortly.

"Where are your notes? I'd like to see them."

January hesitated then drew her notes on the Brauns out of her desk drawer and handed them to him. Attached to the notes were the two pictures of Lance, the childhood photo and the one she'd taken at the recording studio.

"Great photos," Steve said. "You take this?"

She nodded.

"Be good for the cover."

"I gave you cover shots—of the whole group. This is not to be used."

Steve gave her a puzzled look, sat down in a chair, and read through her notes. When he was finished, he slapped them down on her desk. "These are great," he said. "How come you're not using this?"

"Lance asked me not to."

"So?"

"So nothing. I'm going on tour with them. They have to trust me. Especially Lance. If I printed one word of that, it would be over."

"Too bad," Steve said. "It would get him a lot of attention."

"Steve," January protested, "his parents are dead. That kind of attention he doesn't need. Besides, I made a promise."

"And you don't break your promises," said Steve.

"No, I don't," she answered.

Steve glanced at his watch. "It's three o'clock. Why don't you take the rest of the afternoon off? Go home, get packed up. Take tomorrow and the next day off as well. There's nothing here I can't cover. You probably have a lot to do before the trip."

"That," January said, "is the best suggestion I've had all day." She paused. "What about your own story? Is it done?"

"Just about. A few things I have to iron out first."

"I thought they wanted it by noon."

Steve shrugged. "They'll have it by five. I've already talked to them. The page is waiting."

"I'd like to see what you've done so far," she said, suddenly wishing Adrian were here.

"The usual," Steve said smoothly. "A real straight factual piece. Background, high school, that sort of thing. I did some research, not a lot. I didn't have time. That's why I wanted to look at your notes. I'd like to borrow them, as reference."

January reached for them but Steve held them away from her.

"Don't worry," he said. "I won't print anything you don't want printed."

"Lance doesn't want his family name revealed. We have to honor that. I gave my word."

Steve raised his eyebrows. "Honor? January, that's pretty way out. We're running a *news* magazine, remember? And it's our job to give information—the facts—to our readers."

"Fine, but it's my responsibility to win and to keep the confidence of the people I'm going to be on tour with."

Steve smiled easily. "Trust me, January." He spun on his heel and left quickly.

Trust Steve? That was hard to do—but Adrian *had* left him in charge. And she needed the next two days to organize for the trip and get up to Santa Barbara to see her mother. Since her father had died, she'd made a point to spend as much time as she could with her mother. Given her job, that wasn't much time at all. A day here, a day there. But before going on a tour she always tried to see her.

To ease her worries she kept reminding herself that Adrian had left Steve in charge. Adrian trusted him even if she didn't.

Thursday morning, January was dressed and ready to go early. Adrian's wife, Alicia, was picking her up and taking her to the airport.

"Sorry I'm late," Alicia said as she swung into the driveway at the last minute. "Adrian called from Chicago. Is that all you're taking?" she asked as January heaved a duffel bag onto the back seat.

January pointed to her shoulder bag and portable typewriter. "In here, my dear, are camera, miniature tape recorder, paper, the works. I am fully equipped. A walking office."

"I don't know how you stand it," said Alicia. "You and my husband work in the craziest business."

January shrugged. "You have to love it, that's all. How's Adrian?"

"Ecstatic. He's flying home today. That's what he called about. I bring you out to the airport and then I hang around for an hour and pick him up. He says to tell you he loves you, he has a great story on the Stones, and to have a good trip."

January glanced at her watch.

"Don't worry," said Alicia, "We'll make it in time."

"Did you see the new issue of *Offbeat?* I didn't have a chance to get to the office and pick one up. I was with my mother all day yesterday and didn't get back until late last night."

"How was she?"

"Fine. She was a little lonely but I think she's met some guy." January grinned. "Imagine, at her age."

"Ha," Alicia said. "It only shows that she's smarter

than you. At least she's going out."

January groaned. "Don't start on me, Alicia. Between you and Adrian. . . . Speaking of Adrian, did you see the new *Offbeat* or not?"

"I didn't," Alicia said. "Adrian asked me exactly the same question. It hadn't hit the stands in Chicago when he called. He wanted to know how your story came out."

"I liked it. Still, I'm anxious to see it in print."

"You can pick up a copy at the airport."

But there wasn't time at the airport. There was only time to check in, dash through security, typewriter in one hand, oversized bag in the other. Alicia at her side, January ran practically all the way to the gate. She'd see the new *Offbeat* on the plane. Someone in the group was sure to have a copy. Quickly she kissed Alicia goodbye and, clutching everything tightly, boarded the plane. She hadn't seen Lance since Saturday and realized there was a knot of eager anticipation in her stomach. Business, she reminded herself, business. You're on an assignment, Warburton.

The flight attendant stowed her typewriter for her and indicated the four rows of seats toward the back that were taken up by L.A. Expressway and their road crew, or roadies as they were called. Figures, thought January; even Platinum Records can't be bothered to send its bands first class.

She smiled at them as she headed down the aisle. But if any of the band members—Teri, Joel, Derek, or Samson—noticed her, they gave no indication of it. At first she didn't see Lance at all, then spotted him in a window seat. The space beside him was taken. Rick was at his side. The two had their heads bent down and were talking. For a brief moment Lance looked up, saw her, and looked down again.

The seat she'd been assigned was on the side of the plane away from Lance. Next to her was a burly man in a black T-shirt with L.A. EXPRESSWAY written across it.

"You the reporter?" he growled.

She nodded.

He stood up. "All I do is carry equipment for this group. But I'm loyal. I've been with them a long time. I'd appreciate you keeping out of my way." He rose and stalked down the aisle. The plane wasn't full and apparently he was able to locate another seat. He didn't come back.

Teri was in the next row over. January tried to catch her eye, but it was clear that Teri and Joel were both avoiding her. As the plane lifted and the NO SMOKING sign blinked off, January began to worry seriously about what was going on. When half an hour had gone by and not a single member of the group had come over to greet her or had even given any indication that they were aware of her presence, she was determined to find out why she was being treated like a leper. She no longer tried to make eye contact with anyone, but she watched all the band members and especially and surreptitiously she watched Lance. Eventually she saw Rick get up and head toward the restrooms. There was a line, so she knew it would be several minutes at least before he got back. Steeling herself, she went over to Lance.

"Lance," she began.

Before she could say another word, he was on his feet, pushing her out of his way and walking off. She wanted to follow him, but her instincts told her not to. Besides, how far could he go on a plane? He would have to sit down somewhere sooner or later. Was that what they all planned to do—ignore her, not speak to her for the length of the entire tour? And when she didn't even know what she'd done? Resolutely, she took Lance's seat.

When Rick came back, he found her there. "You want something, reporter?" he said coldly.

"I want to know what's going on," she said.

Rick sneered. "Don't give me that, lady. You've done enough. Don't play innocent now."

"What have I done?" January asked evenly. She spoke coolly but loudly. Three seats away, she was aware of Teri listening.

"You planning to stay in that seat?" Rick asked.

"Until I find out what's going on."

Other passengers were craning to look at them.

"Then I'll find another," Rick said.

A flight attendant came up. "Is there some problem, sir?"

"None at all. Just about to get me another seat, that's all."

"There are plenty up front," the woman said. "I believe one of your friends is already up there. He said it was too crowded back here."

"He's right," Rick said. He turned to January. "Lady, I'd like to give you some advice. When this plane lands, stay on it. Take it right back to L.A. or wherever it's going, because I can guarantee that no one in this band is going to speak to you again. And if you try to get anywhere near Lance Devlin, I will personally see to it that you are prevented. Is that clear?"

Before January could respond, Rick had walked away. The flight attendant glanced at her curiously, then followed Rick down the aisle. The other passengers went back to their books and magazines.

January ate her lunch alone and in silence. Every once in a while she'd notice Teri's eye on her as if she were thinking something over. Teri must have made up her mind because as the flight attendants were clearing away the trays she came over, slipping into the seat next to her.

"How could you do it?" Teri asked. "How could you do it to him, to all of us? We trusted you."

January looked Teri straight in the eye. "You must believe me. I have absolutely no idea what you're talking about."

Teri laughed cynically. "Well, then, let me jog your memory." She reached into her handbag, drew out the new issue of *Offbeat*, and tossed it in January's lap.

The cover photo was the black-and-white shot of Lance. In the lower left-hand corner was reprinted the childhood picture of him, innocent and grinning. The headline read: "LANCE DEVLIN (BRAUN!?) HITS THE ROAD AGAIN. IS HE HIS MOTHER'S SON?" And in smaller print it read: "JANUARY WARBURTON GETS THE EXCLUSIVE STORY."

chapter

5

"TERI, I had nothing to do with this, I swear." January's face was white with shock.

"You didn't take that cover photo of Lance?"

"I did, but..."

"And you didn't dig up that whole story?"

"Yes, but..."

Teri turned away in disgust.

"Wait," January said. "You don't understand. You have to listen. Please. Of course I took the picture, and I did find out the story as well, but it wasn't meant to be printed. They were my notes. I made Steve promise..." She paused. "Damn him!" she said vehemently. "How could he? How dare he?"

Hearing the fury in January's voice, Teri turned to look at her. "You really didn't write it?"

61

"Of course not. I promised Lance. I'd never do a thing like that." She was leafing hastily through the magazine. The cover story was in the center. There were two articles, the one she had written, and the one Steve had developed out of her notes. Both stories were accompanied by her photos.

"This is the article I wrote," she said to Teri, tapping her own story with a finger. "This one and only this one. There's my by-line right there," she said, pointing to her name.

"Your name's on both stories," Teri said.

"No," January said, examining the by-line on the other story. "No it's not. It says 'S. C., from notes by January Warburton.' 'S.C.' That means Steve Creighton. He's an associate editor. He kept my notes and went spinning off on his own. I can't believe he did this. Even the cover photo. That was never meant to have appeared. I printed that for myself, not for publication."

"You printed it for yourself?" Teri said. "Why?"

January shrugged. "It's a great picture."

"It is." Teri laughed shortly. "In all his fury, even Lance admitted to that. He'd love to have it on the album cover. Why wasn't it for publication?"

January blushed, embarrassed. "I did it for me, that was all."

"You really like him, don't you?"

"Yes," January said softly. "Yes, I do."

"Then if you feel that way, how could you have ever let this story go out?"

"I didn't," she said. "I had absolutely nothing to do with it. Steve took my notes. He said he wanted to read them through one more time. He was assigned to do the profile on Lance. I explained to him that Lance's background was to be kept a secret, that..." January paused. "It *is* my fault, though. I knew I couldn't trust him. I didn't even want to show him those notes. He's lazy. He'd have never looked up this information in the files himself. If I hadn't left town, if I hadn't gone up to see my mother, but just stayed in the office, checked everything he did . . ." Frustrated, angry, on the verge of tears, January pushed back her seat.

"I don't know what to do," she said. "I don't know how to make amends. I don't blame you all for hating me. The best thing I could do would be to take myself off the story. Right now *I* hate the press." She laughed bitterly. "The irony was that I was going to get Lance to trust the press. Now, he never will."

"So what are you going to do?" Teri asked. "Quit? Give up?"

"What else can I do? Even if you believe me, who else is going to? Certainly not Lance."

"No, Lance you're going to have to win around by yourself. The others will believe me if I tell them you knew nothing about it."

"Why do *you* believe me?" January asked.

Teri covered her hand with her own. "Instincts. I liked you the first time I saw you. I thought you were honest. I still think you are. Besides," she said with a laugh, "if you really were responsible for the story, you'd have never dared get on this plane."

"That's the truth," January said. "Good old Steve didn't even warn me. Sent me right into the lions' den instead, unarmed and with no forewarning. But it was partly my fault. I had a feeling I shouldn't have left him with those notes." She glanced at the story. "I wonder if he got the facts correct. Knowing him, he didn't."

"He didn't," Teri said.

Something in her voice made January look up. "What do you mean?"

Teri spoke angrily. "The missing ingredient in this story is the same as it was fourteen years ago—the truth."

"But . . ."

"Lenora Braun never had an affair with anyone. She was faithful to her husband until the day they died. The press made the whole story up. Beautiful woman, handsome conductor—exactly as it's written here, except that it wasn't true."

"But why would anyone make up a story like that?"

"To sell papers," snapped Teri. "Why else?"

January recalled Steve saying very similar things in the past. He really didn't believe in *facts* at all.

"Lance was a teenager when it all happened," Teri continued. "We were close friends. The papers came out with this story and no matter how much his father supported her, no one believed him. People liked the dirty gossip better."

"But what about that conductor? Why didn't he ever say anything?"

"Oh," said Teri, "he loved it. He always had wanted Lenora. This was the closest he was going to get. He didn't want to deny anything—but he couldn't say it was the truth, either. So he kept silent. You can't imagine what it was like for Lance in high school, all the kids staring at him, saying things behind his back. It was hell. And then when the shock was over, the story finally forgotten, and Lenora and Franz went out in public again, they were killed in that plane crash."

"And then this gets printed."

"And Lance is forced to relive the whole thing all over again," Teri said.

"What can I do?" January asked.

"I don't know. He was willing to trust you before. He liked you. But not anymore. I don't know what you can do."

January and Teri sat side by side, lost in their own thoughts. The hushed cabin, darkened for the in-flight film, only added to January's gloomy mood.

As the wheels of the jet touched ground and the plane cruised down the runway, Teri mentioned the name of the hotel where they were staying.

"I know," January said. "I have a room booked there."

"The bus is picking us up at the airport."

"I'm supposed to travel on the bus with you," January said, biting her lip, "but I think I'll take a cab. Check in separately."

Teri smiled. "Good idea. I'll talk to the guys and explain. We're playing a gig tonight so there'll probably be a sound check as soon as we get into town, but I'll call your room when I can. Hang in there and wait to hear from me."

January nodded and watched as the rest of the band members filed by her. Even Derek wouldn't meet her eye. The copy of *Offbeat* was still in her hands. As the plane emptied, she skimmed through it. It was worse than she could have imagined; turning what she now knew to be the false story about Lance's parents into sordid gossip. Steve Creighton, she thought as she stood up, you just lost your job!

She took her time getting a cab so as to give the band members a chance to get to the hotel and check in well before she arrived. Once at the hotel, she went straight to her room and placed a call to Los Angeles. She could tell by Adrian's voice that he'd been waiting for her call.

"Creighton's already been fired." Adrian spoke roughly and quickly before she could even say a word.

"Adrian, Lance isn't speaking to me. None of them are except Teri."

"Have you explained?"

"Explained!" January cried. "What am I going to say? That we have a second-rate associate editor who will go for the gossip every time? That I'd warned my boss before and he wouldn't listen? You tell me what to say, Adrian, because I don't know."

"Okay," he said. "I deserved that."

But January wasn't finished. "You should never have left the paper in his hands. I told you that. But you didn't want to hear it, did you? I've known all along Creighton was deceitful—*and* that he was going to get us in trouble."

"Hold it," said Adrian. "He only worked up that story from your notes."

"After I made him promise he wouldn't. But that's not the worst of it, Adrian. The worst of it is that the story isn't even true. Lance's mother never had that affair."

"I know," Adrian said.

"You know? How do you know what every other press reporter at the time didn't seem to, or didn't want to?"

"Never mind how I know," he said. "I know. That's all, okay?"

"What about that cover photo? That was *my* photo. It wasn't meant to be released without my permission. Steve had no right . . ."

"Steve's been fired, January!"

"A lot of good that does now. I'm stuck here in Washington on the road with a rock group that hates my guts."

"I'm sorry."

"Sorry's just not good enough." January hung up. She knew Adrian would call back. She paced the floor angrily, trying to decide what to do. As she did, she noticed she hadn't even bothered to shut the door to her room. It was standing wide open. Probably everyone on the corridor had heard her conversation. So what? The phone rang. She gave the door a sharp kick. It flew shut. She picked up the phone. "Yes, Adrian?"

"Are you quitting?"

"No, but I'm tempted."

"What are you going to do?"

"They have a show tonight. I'll see if I can even get in. I suspect all my press passes have been canceled." She could almost hear Adrian thinking.

"Do you want me to call Lance?" he asked at length.

"It might be a good idea. Though I doubt he'll talk to you."

"I think he might. At any rate, I'll give it a try and call you later."

January hung up and plunked down in the room's one armchair. If the band was running a sound check, as Teri had said they would be, then they were all down at the concert hall over at Georgetown University, where they'd be playing for the next three nights. Their instruments would be set up onstage and they'd be testing not only the guitars, pianos, and drums, but the amps, mikes, and acoustics as well. A sound check could take ten minutes or two hours. They'd grab a light meal, a quick rest, and begin to get their energy up for the show. She desperately wanted to be at the concert hall and wait for the chance to talk to Lance. However, until she had talked to Teri and learned what success she'd had in smoothing the way, January knew she should stay put.

She hauled out her typewriter. Her first thought was to write a letter of apology to Lance. But her next thought was even better. Why not make it an open letter to *Offbeat*? A public apology or retraction of some kind was in order. But when her fingers actually began hitting the typewriter keys, she found herself writing out the whole story: her first meetings with Lance, his mysteriousness about his family, his hatred of the press, the information she'd unearthed, the notes she'd made, and how they'd found their way to publication. It was an honest, spontaneous piece of writing and she wondered if Adrian would even print it. First, however, it would have to meet with Lance's approval. Her story ended with the fact that Lenora had never had an affair and with an indictment of sloppy, irresponsible press reporting especially as had been so recently exemplified in *Offbeat*. She clipped the carbon copy to the original and called down to the lobby.

"Is Lance Devlin in?" she asked the clerk, who was extremely cagey until she made him understand her connection with the group.

"I believe the whole band left a few hours ago. None of them has come back. Would you like me to ring for you?"

"No, thanks," said January. "What's his room number? I have to leave something at the door."

The clerk gave her the number. "Oh, Miss Warburton, checking your box, I find an envelope for you. Shall I have it brought up?"

"I'll come down and get it later, thank you." She hung up. She was much too eager to deliver her piece to Lance to worry about an envelope waiting for her.

Lance's room was on her floor, only three doors down. Terrific, she thought ironically. Avoiding each other would be very, very difficult.

She knocked lightly, once. There was no answer. She tried to slip the pages under the door but they were too thick. She was kneeling, thinking she would probably have to leave them with the desk clerk downstairs, when she heard soft footfalls behind her. She glanced up to see Lance gazing down at her.

"Can I help you with something?" he asked coldly.

"Lance . . ." She rose awkwardly to her feet. He made no effort to help her. "I was just leaving this article for you." She held out the pages to him. He didn't take them. "I wanted you to read it before I gave it to Adrian."

"Another article?" He raised one eyebrow. "The last one wasn't sufficient?"

"Lance, please, if you'll only read this. It explains everything."

"I've been hearing explanations all day. From Teri, from Adrian . . ."

"Adrian called?"

"Yes. Do you mind if I go into my room?"

"Sorry," she said, stepping back so he could turn the key in the lock. But before he could open the door, she blocked it again. "Yes I do mind," she said. "How about *my* explanation? How about listening to me, or at least reading this?"

"I've done enough listening today. And reading," he said. "January, move."

"No. Not until you take this."

There was a sparkle in Lance's eyes. For a moment January thought he was on the edge of laughter. "January," he repeated, "move. Because I don't feel like removing you myself, and I could, no matter how much karate you've taken. Get out of my way, let me open my door, and I'll take your article and read it. And you can sit and watch me."

She stepped out of the way.

He opened the door, let her in, took the story, and then locked the door behind them.

His room had a double bed, an armchair, a sofa, a TV, and a small kitchenette. "Make yourself at home," he said, and lay down on the bed.

January perched nervously on the edge of the armchair. If Lance didn't like this story, she was on her way back to L.A., tonight. She tried not to watch him as he read, tried to ignore the rustle of the pages as he turned them.

He read quickly. When he finished, he set them down on the bed beside him. "January," he said, looking at her, "come here."

She walked over to the bed. Before she knew what was happening he had reached up, caught her hand, and pulled her down onto the bed beside him. Tangling his hands in her hair, he brought her mouth to his and started to kiss her.

"Lance," she said breathlessly, pulling away, "what are you doing?"

"Kissing you," he said with a grin. "Don't you like it?"

"But why? I thought..."

"You're always thinking. Did you get your press passes?"

"What are you talking about?" She felt utterly bewildered. The story might have been good, but it wasn't that good.

"I had Teri leave them for you with the desk clerk earlier. There are two. I thought you might like to bring a date," he teased.

"Earlier?" she said, ignoring the mischievous smile. "You mean you'd already..."

"Forgiven you?" He was still holding her hand, not letting her off the bed. "Yup. But it wasn't because of Teri or even Adrian's call. It was you."

"Me?"

"I was walking by your door and overheard you yelling at Adrian on the phone. That's when I knew you weren't responsible for the article." He picked up the pages. "These do help to redeem you, however." He let them fall and began to pull her down closer.

She resisted. "What about the end?"

"The end of what?"

"The article. It's all right?"

"It's fine. Come here."

"No," she said. "You mean even though it has the stuff about your parents in it?"

"Why should I object to that? It's the first time the truth has finally been printed. And you tore *Offbeat* to pieces better than I ever could have."

"You're really not mad anymore?" January's violet eyes studied him seriously.

"I'm really not, he said softly. He drew her closer, but then let go of her hand, holding her with his eyes only. Gently he began to stroke her arms. January couldn't tear herself away from him. She felt mesmerized. His hands moved up over her shoulders, caressing her neck, lifting her hair, and then letting it fall. He cupped her face and slowly drew her down toward him, kissing the sides of her face, her eyelids, finally her mouth.

January's body felt like white-hot steel as he caught her lower lip lightly between his teeth and ran his tongue over it. His hands were all over her body. She felt as if she were being swept into the vortex of a whirlpool, all control gone. Her body of its own accord pressed closer to his. She kissed him back with a passion and a desire that shook her, as if they were lovers returning to each other after a long separation. She felt the lean strength of his sinewy arms and thighs beneath her hands, the hardness of his chest against hers. She made no attempt to stop him as he unbuttoned her blouse, moved his mouth down her body. In the depth of the whirlpool, she heard her own voice murmuring his name over and over. And then behind that sound came another, a short, sharp electronic sound: *Beep beep, beep beep.*

Lance rolled away from her with a groan.

"What is it?" January said.

He held up his watch. "Wristwatch alarm. Do you realize how late it is? I have to get ready. We go on in an hour and a half. I have to get showered and dressed." He rolled over onto his side, propped himself up with one elbow. "Don't," he said as January started to refasten the buttons of her shirt. "I like to look at you." He bent his head to her breasts again and January felt her body straining toward him once more, as if begging for his lips and tongue. His hand moved over her flat stomach to the snap of her jeans, flicking it open. Abruptly he pulled away. "Can't," he said. "Not now. Not like this."

Dizzy, January opened her eyes to see Lance looking at her, his face close to hers, his green eyes warm and serious.

"I want to make love to you," he said, "but not like this. Not rushed. I want time, the whole night. I want it to be right." He stood up. "You don't know how lovely you are."

January watched him as he pulled his shirt off and went into the bathroom to shower. Slowly she sat up, buttoning her blouse. She gathered up the pages of her article that were scattered on the bed and then sat there, feeling shaky. She didn't know what she wanted. She hadn't expected this, hadn't expected Lance ever to touch her again. And when he had, she had been totally unable to control her feelings. She knew that this time she would have given herself to Lance, and it shocked her. She couldn't even honestly say she was in love with him. She only knew that every time he touched her, all her reason and rationale dropped away. There was nothing but the feel of him, the touch, the closeness, and the desire for more.

She picked up the article and left his room, closing the door quietly behind her. She walked down the corridor to her own room, let herself in, and sat down, waiting for the sensuous trembling of her body to subside. Minutes later the phone rang. It was Lance.

"Where'd you go? Aren't you coming over to the concert hall with me? We can grab a bite to eat before we go if you like."

January shook her head, and then realized Lance couldn't see her. "No," she said, "I'll meet you there. I'll see you after the show."

"Is something wrong?" he asked, concern in his voice.

"No," she said, knowing she needed time to think. "No, nothing. It's only that I'd like to see your first show fresh, as part of the audience. You know?" It was partly true.

"Okay. You sure nothing's wrong? You're not upset about what just happened?"

"Confused, maybe, but not upset."

"January, I want you to know I...damn, hold on, someone's at the door." Lance was gone a few seconds and then returned. "It's Rick. I've gotta go. I'll see you tonight after the show, okay?"

Lance hung up without waiting for her answer. January dialed Adrian's home number.

"I have a story for you," she said. "Take this down, and don't change a word, not a comma, not a period." She read him the article.

When she finished, Adrian said, "So did you two work it out? You and Lance make peace?"

January smiled. "Oh yes, we made peace."

Adrian waited for her to say something more. When she didn't, he added, "You still mad at me?"

"No, but don't ever leave town again. Not even for Mick Jagger."

"Yes, ma'am. Anything else?"

January laughed. "Nope. Just do a good job on my story."

"Guaranteed. And January? After this, use our New York office to phone in articles, okay? They'll telex them. This method is too expensive."

January really laughed this time. "Adrian, you've gotten off easy."

"True," he said. "Have a good time at the concert tonight."

"I intend to," January said. She smiled to herself as she hung up.

chapter

6

THE GEORGETOWN UNIVERSITY auditorium was packed.
Someone had done good advance promotion, or else
L. A. Expressway had a bigger following than January
had realized. Her seats were excellent—third row center.
There was another fifteen minutes before the show was
scheduled to start, which could mean, knowing rock concerts, an actual twenty-five minutes.

January did as she often did at shows she was meant
to cover: hung out with the audience, picked up local
color, sensed the atmosphere. Most of the people present
were young, college age, a mixture representing the various prestigious D.C. colleges and universities. Inter-
mingled was a good smattering of high schoolers. Some
things surprised January. One was the anticipatory feeling in the air. The audience knew who they'd come to

see and they were excited, eager. The other was the number of people in their thirties, an age group that considered itself very much the progenitors of rock, but a group that had become wary about what bands they spent their money on. They were a more finicky, more demanding audience and only turned out for the best. Lance had a reputation for being a great live performer, really catching hold of his audience and sweeping them along with him.

If he's half as good on stage as he is off, January thought with an ironic smile, he'll do just fine.

As the time for the concert's start grew closer, January found herself getting excited, caught up in the atmosphere. She was nervous, too. She wanted Lance to be good. She wanted him to be great. It was a struggle to maintain the fine balance that, as a reporter, she must have—the ability to be caught up emotionally, and yet at the same time keep her objectivity and critical faculties working.

She'd given her extra press pass to a young girl waiting outside the auditorium, obviously hoping against hope to get in. The teenager smiled gratefully and followed January to their seats, saying eagerly how much she loved Lance. She had both of his albums.

"I can't believe I'm here," she sighed joyfully and then sank back into her seat, hands clasped, eyes not leaving the stage for a second.

Roadies sauntered across the stage, checking the amps, setting a guitar in place. Lights were adjusted. The audience leaned forward. There was a murmur, a rush of excitement, a whisper, silence, and then thunderous applause, cheers, and whistles as one by one the group filed out and took their places. Lance, last to come out, strode easily to center stage and grinned out at his audience, shielding his eyes against the light with one hand.

January knew there wasn't a girl in the audience who didn't feel he was looking directly at her.

The applause died down. Lance stood one second longer, then in a motion both fluid and swift, he bent, picked up his guitar, slung the strap around his neck, and hit a chord. At the same instant Samson came in on drums, and they were off.

Lance held the audience the whole way. The energy, the tension never flagged. Even January found herself cheering. And when the band went quiet, when the number was a slow one, once again the audience was right there, listening intently. When Lance introduced his musicians midway through the show, the applause for them was not mere politeness but exuberant enthusiasm.

He's good, thought January again and again, he's good. He's even better than I imagined. For the first time in a long time she felt excited, and blessed Adrian for giving her this job. Being in on the ground floor when a person was about to take off, become a superstar, was always an amazing feeling, one that could send goose bumps up the arms. Being the reporter covering the story of a rising star was the most one could ask for in January's line of work.

Near the end of the concert, the lights dimmed; a single spot was turned on Lance. "I'd like to dedicate this song to someone in the audience. She's going to be traveling with us for a while and she'll be hearing a lot of our music. I hope she doesn't get bored."

He spoke in a slow, easy drawl with a disarming smile on his face. The audience laughed softly. Heads turned. People strained to see to whom the song might have been dedicated. Lance and the band went into "Diamonds of the Sea." This time as Lance sang, January felt a tingling warmth spreading through her body and remembered that afternoon on the bed, the feel of Lance. She closed her eyes, let the music penetrate, and then opened them abruptly. Warburton, she warned herself, you're falling for him, and that's not good.

It was also, she suspected, as the song came to an end, too late.

She was touched by what Lance had done. She knew that everyone in the band would know that it was to her he'd dedicated the song. It was public acceptance, a gesture of peace. Still, she thought, he hadn't yet had to deal with the press on the subject of the *Offbeat* story. After the concert, he would. It was doubtful that at the end of a barrage of reporters' questions and microphones thrust in his face he'd be feeling so charitable toward her. Earlier, on her way to the concert, she'd stopped for a copy of *The Washington Post*. There'd been a mention of Lance's show and a reference to the *Offbeat* article. The rest of the article had been on Franz and Lenora Braun, how they had often performed in Washington, even once appearing before the President, and how the later scandal had destroyed their careers. There was a great deal of curiosity about their rock-star son, Lance Devlin, who until now had managed to keep his identity well hidden.

January wondered if Lance had seen the article. She suspected he hadn't. And was afraid he would.

The band received two callbacks. The audience was on its feet whistling and cheering at the end of the show.

"Come on," whispered January to the girl to whom she'd given her extra pass, "we're going backstage. Let's go before the crowd starts moving." Lance was just finishing up what January knew would be the last song.

The young girl radiated delight. "Really?" she whispered back. "You're taking me backstage?"

January grinned and nodded. Grabbing the teenager's hand, she led her down the row of people, out into the aisle, and hurried her out of the auditorium. The girl was straining at January's hand trying to get one last look at Lance.

January laughed. "You'll see him face to face in a few minutes." She showed one of the ushers her press passes stamped with the words "ADMIT ONE BACKSTAGE." The usher nodded and told them where to go. As they reached the door, the main doors of the auditorium opened and the audience started pouring out. One last look back showed ushers and security guards preventing anyone from getting to the backstage door.

The girl clutched January's hand tightly. January glanced at the tense, excited face. "What's your name," she said, "so I can introduce you."

"Rosie," the girl said, "Rosie Moore."

There was the usual crowd backstage—road crew packing away various instruments; various celebrities; girls who had managed to sneak back despite the ushers; some press. The band members were still in their dressing rooms, calming down, cooling off, changing their clothes. Everyone else was gathered in one large room waiting for them. Ice, wine, beer, Perrier, and plastic glasses were on a table against the wall. January poured Perrier for both her and Rosie, trying for the moment to keep them both in the shadows. There were a few press people whom she recognized and she was afraid if they saw her, they'd question her about the article.

Rick spotted January almost immediately and walked up to her. "Lance wants to see you," he said curtly. "He told me to watch for you. Come on." He turned on his heel and started out of the room.

"Wait," said January. "What about her?" she asked, meaning Rosie.

"Who's she?"

"A friend of mine. She came to the show with me."

"I can wait here," said Rosie. "It's okay. You go."

"No," said January. "You're my guest tonight."

"Both of you, then," said Rick. "Come on."

The dressing room was two doors down. January was relieved to see that there wasn't too much graffiti. Backstage at concert halls could get downright raunchy. University halls tended to be the cleanest.

Rick rapped once on the dressing room door. "January," he announced and pushed it open.

Lance, changed from his stage costume of leather pants and skin tight T-shirt, was in faded jeans and a black cotton shirt. Seated on a wooden chair, his feet propped on another, he was tilted back against the wall, resting. As January came in, he brushed hair out of his eyes and smiled up at her. "How was it?"

"Terrific," she said. "Excellent. Everyone loved you."

He grinned. "Did you like your song?"

Rosie's eyes, which had already been staring intently at Lance as if to memorize every detail of him, widened even more. "That song was for you?" she said to January, awestricken

"It sure was," said Lance, smiling easily. "Who are you?"

It was January's turn to grin. "My date," she said. "The extra pass. This is Rosie Moore. I found her outside wishing she could get in, so I brougl.t her."

Lance looked at January seriously. "That was a really nice thing to do," he said.

She shrugged. "I knew how she felt," she said simply. "I remember once standing in line for hours for Beatles tickets. I didn't get them."

"How'd you like the concert, Rosie Moore?" Lance asked.

"I loved it," the girl said shyly. "I have all your albums."

Lance laughed. "All two of them. Okay, well here's something else to add to your collection." He reached into a cardboard box, pulled out a T-shirt with "LANCE DEVLIN AND L. A. EXPRESSWAY" silkscreened on it. With a black magic marker, he signed his name on it and gave it to Rosie.

"It's a size large," January protested.

"It doesn't matter," Rosie said. "I can wear it as a dress. No one's going to believe this," she murmured. "I can't even believe it."

Lance laughed. "They'll believe the shirt. They'll never believe this," and he gave her a quick kiss on the cheek.

Rosie's cheeks turned bright red.

"Listen," Lance said to January, "there are a whole bunch of people waiting out there for me. In a few minutes Rick is going to be banging the door down and dragging me out. I'm going to make it as quick as I can. Would you..." he stood up and walked over to her, taking her hands in his, "would you go back to the hotel and wait there for me? I'm starving. As soon as I can get out of here, I'd like to have a quiet, late night dinner, just the two of us. We can eat at the hotel, or go out. Whatever you like."

"I really ought to be there when the press interviews you. It is my job." January's protest was weak. All she was conscious of was Lance's hands holding hers, the steady warmth of his eyes, the closeness of him. Dimly she was aware of Rosie watching them.

"I won't tell them anything," Lance said.

"But..."

"But what?" He put a finger to her lips.

She wished suddenly, fervently that they were alone together, that his arms were around her, his lips against hers.

As if reading her mind, he took a step closer and then seemed to remember Rosie. He cleared his throat. "But what?"

"The press. You never saw *The Washington Post* story. The *Offbeat* article—it's everywhere. They're all talking about it, and your parents."

"I did see the article in the *Post*," Lance said. "Don't worry. I can handle it."

"But it was my fault. I'd like to be there, to explain."

"The explanation'll come out soon enough. In the meantime, I'm not answering any questions. None. So don't worry. If you really want to do something for me, go back to the hotel and wait for me there. I'll call your room as soon as I get back. A half hour. No more. Okay?" he said.

"Okay," she answered, wishing she didn't have misgivings.

"Rosie," Lance said, "do you have a way home?"

"My mother told me to call after the concert and she'd pick me up."

"I'll take you home in a cab," January offered. "Where do you live?"

"Georgetown. M Street," the girl answered.

"No problem," January said. She turned back to Lance. "You're sure you don't want me to stay?"

"Sure," he said. "Go. I'll see you in half an hour." He kissed her lightly on the mouth and then gave Rosie another kiss on the cheek. "Night, ladies," he said with a grin.

Rick was at the door as January went out. "Lance," he said, "they're waiting." He gave January a surly look but held the door for her.

On their way out, Rosie asked, "He really likes you, doesn't he?"

"Who? Lance? I guess," said January, unsure herself.

"Is he your boyfriend?"

January laughed. "No."

"Is he going to be?"

"I don't know," January said, not daring to even think about it.

"Well, I think he's going to be." Rosie hugged her T-shirt. "Wait till everyone sees this at school tomorrow. They are going to be so jealous."

"Your mother actually left you here by yourself?"

"Well, some friends of mine had tickets and she said if I didn't get in to call her and she'd come get me, otherwise to call her after the show."

"We better get you home now, then, so she doesn't get worried about you." January hailed a cab, and Rosie gave the address.

After letting the girl off and seeing that she was home safe with her family, January gave the cabbie the address of the hotel. The cab driver was young, paying his way through school. "You go to see Lance Devlin and L. A. Expressway tonight?" he asked conversationally.

January nodded. "Yes," she said.

"That hotel you're at—that's where they're staying, isn't it? I heard they were real good. Their concert sold out tonight. How come you're in the same hotel? You from out of town?"

"L.A.," answered January.

"Not a reporter, are you?"

"As a matter of fact, I am."

"What did you think of that story in *Offbeat*?" The driver glanced at her through the rear-view mirror. "I didn't like it much myself, digging into Lance Devlin's past like that. His family at that. What's all that got to do with his music? I was surprised. *Offbeat* doesn't usually print stuff like that, and that writer, January What's-her-name, she's usually pretty good."

"I didn't like the article at all," January said honestly.

The cab pulled up at the hotel. "Who do you work for?" the driver asked as she paid him.

"Offbeat," she said with a smile.

"Hey, you're not..."

"I am," January said, taking her change and giving him a dollar tip.

"Oh boy," the driver said.

"But I didn't write that article. Check out the next issue. It'll be out in two weeks." January sounded cheerful as she spoke, but as she walked up the steps to the hotel lobby, she was angry. She didn't like having to take the blame for something she'd never written or even authorized.

There were no messages for her at the desk, and her anger dissipated as she took the elevator up to her floor. She glanced at her watch. It was eleven-thirty. Midnight dinners were nothing unusual on the road.

In her room, she ran a comb through her hair, freshened her make-up, and added a little scent. She left on her maroon velvet jeans but exchanged the dark cotton jersey for a soft white silk blouse. During the concert, she has spoken quietly into her tape recorder, listing the songs Lance did and in what order, making occasional notes or comments as they occurred to her on the music itself or the audience and general atmosphere. Now, waiting for Lance's call, she listened to the tape, transcribing the material into a notebook. Later she would write it all up into a story. For the moment she was gathering information.

It was exactly midnight when she finished. She had a paperback novel with her, and lay down on her bed to read while waiting for Lance's call or knock.

At one, she had still heard nothing from him. She rationalized that he might have had to go out to dinner unexpectedly or that, too tired, he had come back and gone straight to bed. But she couldn't rationalize his failure at least to call her and let her know what was going on. Slowly she undressed, washed her face, and slipped into the oversized shirt she always slept in when on the road. She told herself as she got into bed that she didn't care, it was just as well this way. To get involved with Lance Devlin was foolish, and the sooner it all came to an end the better. Still, before turning out her light, she couldn't resist calling the desk downstairs and asking if Lance had come back in. The clerk answered that he hadn't.

Damn him anyway, she said to herself, burying her face in her pillow. It's your own fault, she told herself, letting yourself be so easily seduced by a rock musician. You should know better.

But all the self-chastising in the world didn't make her sleep any easier. Every sound—cars outside her window or people in the hall—woke her up and made her listen. The glowing numbers on her travel alarm said three-fifteen when she finally heard Lance.

"How about one more beer, man?" said Rick's voice in the hall outside her room.

"Sleep, I need some sleep," Lance said.

"You can sleep all day tomorrow. Come on, I got beer in my room. Samson's already there."

January couldn't hear what Lance answered. And then he cursed softly. "I never called January. You were supposed to remind me."

"Yeah," Rick said, "sorry. Anyway, she's just a reporter. What do you care?"

Again Lance's reply was muffled. The voices disappeared. A door slammed. The hotel went quiet, and January once more pulled the pillow over her head. What *does* he care, she thought. Just a reporter. Exactly. "Thanks, Rick," she muttered, "thanks for helping me get it straight."

chapter

7

JANUARY was up early the next morning, despite the three-hour time difference and the lack of sleep. She consulted her tour schedule. They had three days in Washington, then on to Philadelphia, New Haven, Providence, Boston, and finally New York for the huge benefit concert at Madison Square Garden. They would be spending three days in each city, giving two to three concerts per place. If the group managed to maintain the high level of energy and fine quality of last night's show, then Lance Devlin and L.A. Expressway were going to be a smash success in the east.

It had been a long time since January had been in Washington. It was a city she loved, for the elegance of its architecture, its cosmopolitan atmosphere, its culture and beauty. It was a habit of hers to keep a list of things she wanted to see in various cities for such occasions as these—when she was on the road and had some time to herself. The last time she'd been in Washington, she'd seen the major sights: the White House, the Washington Monument, the Lincoln Memorial, the Smithsonian, and the National Gallery. This time she wanted to walk around Georgetown and then see some of the smaller galleries. There was one in particular, the Phillips Memorial Gallery, that she'd heard of often and never been to.

An hour later, she was comfortably seated in a small French-style cafe in the heart of Georgetown sipping espresso and eating a flaky croissant dripping with honey and butter. The atmosphere, the busy street, the smell of European coffee, reminded her of Paris and the four days she'd spent there with Mike on their honeymoon. She realized it had been a while since she'd thought of Mike at all. Lance had wiped him right out of her mind. It was no wonder, she thought ironically, that this morning Mike would be on her mind again. It hadn't been long into their marriage, those idyllic days in Paris scarcely left behind, that Mike had started coming in at all hours of the morning—if he had come in at all, she reminded herself bitterly. At first she had believed him when he said it was business. "P.R." had been his expression—"got to keep the clients happy." She'd accepted that until she'd seen a few pictures of him with his so-called clients. Things had come to a rapid halt soon after that.

And now similar patterns seemed to be starting all over again with Lance. And they weren't even lovers, she thought, not to speak of married. She wondered for the first time if her father's death hadn't affected her more than she'd realized. Perhaps she chose men who were going to leave her.

But no, she thought, her father had been an utterly trustworthy, warm, loving man. People like Mike and Lance were completely different—making promises, setting dates, and then not keeping them. Fortunately things hadn't gone too far with Lance; far enough, however, for her to know they had to come to an end now. She would not, she vowed to herself, go through with him what she had been through with Mike. The least she could do was learn from her mistakes.

The Phillips Gallery was everything she'd imagined it would be and more. It was an old brown house formerly privately owned. The house and its collection of paintings was now open to the public. January liked seeing a fine art collection in a home instead of a cold museum. It was a good reminder that paintings were done to be lived with, not just viewed and walked away from. Many of the works by masters such as Goya and El Greco overwhelmed her, but the one she actually sat down in front of, the one that gave her a feeling of light and joy, was one by Renoir.

It was *Luncheon of the Boating Party*, and it was much larger than she'd imagined it would be. It was big enough so that sitting gazing at it, she actually felt she was there, at the table, drinking wine, leafy green around her, an awning overhead. She felt she could almost hear the conversation of the young men and women in their straw hats and summery clothes.

"Beautiful, isn't it?" a voice behind her said.

"Yes," she said softly, not even turning to see who had spoken, knowing only that it had been a male voice.

"It's always been my favorite. My mother used to bring me here when I was a boy, whenever she and my father played here."

January realized she knew the voice. Startled, she turned around.

Lance seemed to take their unexpected meeting as perfectly natural. He was standing behind her, leaning slightly back, arms folded over his chest, looking at the painting as he talked to her. "It was my mother's favorite, too. I always thought she and my father looked sort of like those two." He pointed to a woman seated at the table, a man behind her, leaning over her shoulder, speaking to her. The woman's face was turned up to his.

"It's been a long time since I looked at this painting," Lance said. "This is the third or fourth time I've been back to D.C. since they died, but I always avoided this gallery. Today I woke up and decided it was time. Where were you this morning?" he asked abruptly, coming around and sitting down beside her.

"Where was I?" January said.

"I came to your room at nine o'clock. You were already gone."

"You didn't get much sleep, did you?" January blurted out.

Lance grinned at her. "How would you know? Were you waiting up for me?"

"You made so much noise coming in, you woke me up. Besides," she snapped, "if you remember, we had a date. Oh, never mind," she said, standing up. "Let's not even discuss it."

He grabbed her shoulder bag, preventing her from leaving. "Wait a minute. Discuss what?"

"Nothing. I should have known, that's all."

"Known what?" Lance said. "Look, about last night, I'm really sorry. I wanted to have dinner with you. I tried to get back, but our press agent, Diane, had flown in from L.A. She was there last night. We had to get a few things straight with the press, and then after that I had to go to a party. I was so tired I couldn't see straight. I just ate the food and drank the wine and tried to stay awake. Rick got me home."

"I know," January said shortly. "I heard him."

"I tried to call," Lance said. "First from the auditorium, but you hadn't gotten home yet, then from the house where we were."

January felt like she was listening to an instant replay of one of Mike's excuses. She didn't even want to hear it. "There weren't any messages," she said.

"I know," he said. "When I couldn't get you the first time I figured I'd call later, so I didn't leave a message with the desk clerk. And when I tried to phone you from that house, someone was always on the phone or else wanting to talk to me or something."

"It doesn't matter," January said, trying to turn away.

"It matters to me," Lance said, standing up and forcing her to look at him. "You think I'm making excuses—that I simply forgot."

"I heard you in the hall," January said wearily. "You were telling Rick he'd forgotten to remind you to call."

"At one o'clock," Lance said, "even though I thought you'd be asleep. Never mind," he said. "I'm not going to stand here all day apologizing. What are you doing here, anyway? I came here to be alone."

"So did I," January snapped.

Abruptly they both burst out laughing.

"Well, now that we're both here," Lance said, "what do you want to do?"

"I don't know," she said.

Lance took a last look at the painting. "Let's start by getting out of here."

They spent the whole day together. Much as January hated to admit it, it was one of the nicest, most relaxed days she'd ever spent with anyone.

"Diane is going to be furious," Lance said around three o'clock as they finished a late lunch.

"Why?" January asked, feeling slightly giddy from white wine and the pleasure of being with Lance.

"There was some promo thing I was supposed to be at about an hour ago." He glanced at his watch.

"What kind of promo thing?" January said, trying to sound concerned, but stifling a giggle all the same.

"I don't know. Some senator talking about something. I was to show up and support him and then it would be in the papers and everyone would come to the show and he'd get votes."

"Oh dear," January sighed, "that's terrible," and then the giggle erupted despite herself.

Lance looked at her and started to laugh. "Terrible," he agreed, and they laughed harder. "January," he said seriously.

"What?"

He studied her face a few minutes thoughtfully. "Nothing," he said.

There were a few moments of silence. "Perhaps we should go back to the hotel," he said.

"Perhaps we should," she answered.

They walked back hand in hand.

"How is it," January asked, "that every time I get really mad at you and decide to have nothing to do with you, I end up liking you all over again?"

Lance put an arm around her. "Because I'm irresistible."

"Besides that."

"Because fundamentally I'm a nice, honest guy."

"Really?"

"Really."

"Then why don't I trust you?" she asked.

"Because you don't trust any man," he said, holding open the main door of the hotel for her.

"That's not true," January said as they got in the elevator.

"Oh no?" he said.

"No," she said, ducking as he tried to kiss her.

The elevator stopped. The doors slid open.

"No one's here," Lance said. "None of the band. Rick isn't either. They've all gone to that lunch thing."

"Rick doesn't like me."

They were walking down the hall.

"Nope," Lance said.

Past January's room.

"Why not?" she asked.

To Lance's room. He unlocked the door and ushered her in. "Because he still thinks you crossed me. And because he doesn't like reporters any more than I do, probably less."

"That's all right," January said teasingly, "I don't like rock musicians."

"No?" Lance said as he closed the door.

"No," January said as he kissed her.

"Not at all?" Lance said, leading her toward the bed.

"Sometimes," she said softly as he kissed her neck, "just a little."

"How much," he said, pinning her arms down and teasing her skin delicately with his lips, "could you like me?" He lowered his body onto hers and raised her shirt over her breasts. His hands stroked the soft curved flesh; his fingertips grazed her hardening nipples. His mouth felt like it was blazing trails of fire over her skin. "How much?" he whispered.

"A lot," she murmured, wanting to feel him still closer; the length of his body against hers, skin to skin.

He unfastened the thin cotton skirt she was wearing and slid it down over her hips. Late afternoon sunlight streamed through the window, warming the bed, gilding their bodies. Lance's fingers were light, the touch of a summer breeze, making her tremble like the ruffled surface of a clear pond. He undressed slowly, giving her time to know his body.

January knew she'd never felt like this before. Sex with Mike had been passionate but somehow lacking in emotion, callous after the first few times. She'd never known this tender, inflaming concern. Lance made her feel that the parts of her body were delicate petals of flowers unfurling. Yet a river was rushing through her, sweeping her into its current.

"Tell me you want me," he murmured.

His hands seemed to be on every part of her all at once. She didn't know where her body left off and his began.

"I want you," she whispered. "I want you, Lance," knowing she could no longer deny it to herself or him.

The river that held them was dark, mysterious, pounding through her veins, setting every nerve ending throbbing. She felt bound to him, as if they were one body, one being.

"Tell me you love me, January," he whispered. "Say it."

For a moment she was aware of the deep green of his eyes, his face over hers, an intensity in his expression that shook her. "I love you," she said, the words breaking out almost in a sob. And then there was darkness and the river rushing forward, surging into the ocean, and the ocean receiving it; everything merged, blended into one.

January opened her eyes slowly to sunlight and Lance holding her closely, his eyes gentle and tender. "Ssh," he said, "Don't move, don't say a word. I want to look at you like this." His tongue flicked at her lashes. "You're always crying," he said softly. He smiled. "Salty," he said. "Do you always cry when you make love?"

January shook her head, her dark hair spread out over the pillow. "I never did before."

Lance gathered her in closer. "How long had it been since you'd made love?"

"Not since I was married," January confessed. She ran a hand down his muscled back. "It was worth the wait," she said with a smile.

He raised up from her. "Are you ready for more?" There was laughter in his eyes, as warm as the sunlight.

January felt her body's immediate and urgent response. "Yes," she said, her eyes filled with laughter and desire. "Yes," she said, drawing him back down. "I do believe I am."

Hours later, they awoke to darkness outside and the sound of pounding on the door.

"Lance, are you in there? It's me, Rick. Come on, man, wake up. You got a show to do tonight."

Lance groaned and rolled away from January. He slid into his jeans and went to the door, opening it a crack.

"What's going on?" January heard Rick say. "You got a girl in there? Big deal. Since when did you hide them? Come on. Where've you been all day? Diane was ready to kill."

"Sorry," said Lance. "What time is it?"

"Seven-thirty. Show starts at nine. Let's get going."

"Okay, okay." Lance ran a hand through his hair. "Be with you shortly."

"Hey, you seen that girl reporter around? Diane

wanted to talk to her. 'Bout that *Offbeat* trash. You gotta get rid of that chick, Lance. We can't have her on the road with us. She's only going to make trouble."

"Who? Diane?"

"No, come one. You know who I mean. January. You seen her?"

"I haven't seen her all day," said Lance.

"Okay, well, if you do, tell her Diane's looking for her."

"Right." Lance shut the door and turned back to January, who was sitting up on the bed, a sheet wrapped around her. Lance flicked on a desk lamp, studied her for several minutes, and then took two steps and leaped onto the bed, landing practically on top of her. "Anyone seen January?" he teased, tickling her just below the ribs.

"Stop, Lance," she cried, laughing and trying to roll away.

"Anyone seen the most beautiful girl in the world?" he said, not letting her go.

"Don't," she gasped.

"Don't, do. Yes, no. Contradictions. That's all you ever speak—contradictions!" He tore the sheet away and gazed at her body, making her feel suddenly shy. "I ought to take you onstage exactly like this and show the whole world how beautiful you are. Are you going to take a shower with me?"

"Yes," she said.

"Then come on."

In the shower, water streamed down their bodies. Lance soaped January's hair, watched the white suds slide down over her shoulders and breasts.

"I wish I didn't have to work tonight," he said. "I wish we could spend the whole evening together—have dinner, go back to bed. Are you coming to the concert tonight?"

"Of course," said January. "That's my job."

"Aha," he said, "Then it's not my brilliant music that lures you."

"That too," she said.

He turned off the water and, grabbing a towel, began to rub her down, massaging her body briskly. "Meet me after the show," he said. "In my dressing room. I promise we'll have dinner together after, no matter what. I won't let you out of my sight. Do you love me?"

"Don't ask me that," January said.

"You said you did once before."

"In the heat of passion."

"You do love me," Lance said. "You can't help it. I'm irresistible."

"Oh shut up," said January, twisting away from him. "You have an ego bigger than Mount Rushmore."

Lance grinned. "But you love me."

"Sometimes," January said. "Only once in a great while. Mostly I find you impossible. Get dressed. I'm going to my room. I'll see you after the show."

Lance was trying to whistle as he shaved. "I'm going to be great tonight," he called after her as she went back to the bedroom. "All for you."

"You better be," January yelled back as she slipped into her clothes, "because, don't forget, I'm still the press."

Lance leered out at her from the bathroom, foamy white shaving cream all over his face. "Best press I ever had," he said.

He ducked the shoe that January sent hurtling toward him.

Grinning, she left his room and went down to her own. She'd hardly been in it five minutes when there was a knock at the door. Expecting Lance, she flung it open, saying, "Haven't you had enough?"

A dark-haired woman, very good looking, dressed in expensive, tailored clothes confronted her. "Just about," she said, taking in at a glance January's damp hair and disheveled clothes. "Am I disturbing you?"

"No," January said, recognizing from photos and occasional parties the press agent Diane Maitland. She was both younger and better looking than January had realized.

"I don't suppose you know where Lance has been all day?" Diane asked, pushing her way in and taking the one armchair.

"Why should I?" January said.

"You seem to know everything else about him, Miss Warburton."

"Ms.," January corrected. "Why do you say that?"

"Your article was uncalled for," Diane said, ignoring the question. "It could have done Lance a lot of harm."

"It wasn't my article..."

"So I've been told. At any rate, we're making it work for us. I hear you have another article coming out in two weeks—a retraction of sorts. I'd like to read it."

"You can't," January said flatly. "You may be his press agent, but that's all. You do not control the press itself."

"Lance says he read it."

"I felt I owed him that much."

"Ms. Warburton," Diane said, "are you going to work with me or not?"

"I am going to do my job. Whether that works for or against you depends on the quality of Lance's and the group's music—nothing else."

"Between us we could make Lance into a superstar," Diane said softly.

"Lance *is* a superstar—potentially. If he realizes that potential, his fans will see it."

Diane gave her an acute look. "I wouldn't get any ideas about him. I can see he's already won you, but I warn you, Lance can get a girl to say 'I love you' in two seconds flat." She laughed a cynical little laugh, as if she knew something January didn't. "Love them and leave them—that's Lance's motto. He only remains true to the people who work with him: myself, his band, Rick. If you want him in your life, you better write good reviews."

January held her tongue, wondering silently how much she could write about Lance's entourage. They were not, most of them, the friendliest of people.

"Lance is very ambitious," Diane continued, ignoring January's stony expression. "Why do you think he has been courting you? Good press, Ms. Warburton, that's what he's after—and he'll get it any way he can." Diane stood up. "Your hair's still damp. Did I get you out of the shower? I'm sorry. I could have sworn I saw you coming down the hall from Lance's room several minutes ago. I've got to be going. Thank you for your time."

"No problem," January muttered as the door swung closed behind Diane.

Abruptly January sat down. What if everything Diane said was true? That Lance was using her to get good reviews. She didn't want to believe it—she *couldn't* believe it! How could the exquisite beauty of their love-making, the marvelous fun of their playing together be false on his part? So wonderful . . . tears stung her eyes. So wonderful for *her,* but what about Lance? Was there any chance at all that he really could be using her? She winced. Diane's taunting words came with a rush into her mind. Yes. He got the words *I love you* out of her. She'd never heard them from his lips.

A knocking roused her from these painful thoughts. She opened the door more cautiously this time, unsure if she wanted it to be Lance or not. It was Teri.

"Hi," the blonde singer said. "I haven't had a chance to see you at all. I thought I'd check on how you were doing. Was that Diane I saw leaving here?"

January nodded.

"What did she want? Causing trouble, I suppose." Teri flopped down on the bed. "We've got to get a new press agent. That woman makes life impossible for everyone. Boy, Lance was lucky he missed that lunch today. It was awful. Except the food." She rubbed her stomach. "The food was great—lobster Newberg. You don't know where Lance was, do you? He always wanders off in cities. Goes to galleries." Teri laughed. "Underneath that supercool surface is this terribly sensitive creature."

"He was with me," January said, suddenly welcoming

the opportunity to talk. For whatever reasons, she trusted
Teri.

"Really?" Teri said. "That's great. What did you do?"

"We met accidentally, had lunch..."

"Yeah, he was upset last night. He kept trying to get
you on the phone. Then Rick was supposed to call and
blew it. Typical Rick. He means well but he has this
attitude that everyone has to be kept away from Lance
except, you know, one-night stands."

Then he did try to call, January thought, relieved.

"So what did you do this afternoon?"

"Um, well, we came back here and just sort of, uh,
you know..."

Teri laughed. "Yeah, I know. Never mind. End questions. Look, I came by to tell you that I'm glad you two
are working things out. Lance is a very special person—
loyal, loving." Teri's eyes narrowed. "I'd sure hate to
see him get hurt."

January shook her head. "One minute Diane is telling
me Lance thinks only of his career, is all ambition. Then
you're telling me how sweet he is."

"So," Teri said, sitting up, "judge him for yourself."
She clambered off the bed. "I gotta go. Show time." She
put a hand on January's arm. "Lance is special. Believe
me. We've known each other our whole lives. People
like Diane—they're the ones who are greedy and ambitious. They can't admit to it, so they try to lay it all
on somebody else's doorstep. Trust your feelings."

But her feelings, she thought as Teri left, were all
mixed up. The only thing she was sure of was that the
afternoon she had spent with Lance was the best in her
life. What she had felt with him, she had felt with no
other man. Trust your feelings, Teri said. He loves them
and leaves them, Diane said. Had Diane been left? Was
she jealous?

January shook her head. Mike had made her cautious,
too cautious. She'd do as Teri advised: trust. Perhaps
this time it might really work out.

Feeling better, she changed for the evening's show and her later date with Lance, then headed over to the concert hall.

The show went well, as well as anyone could hope. The auditorium was once again packed, the audience even more enthusiastic than the one the night before. The band wasn't quite as precise on a couple of numbers but Lance's voice soared out, full and rich, and Teri matched him note for note, the perfect complement. By the end of the show, the audience was on its feet, clapping and stomping and yelling for more.

This time, January decided to stay until the audience had filed out so she could hear their comments. Most of what she heard was positive. The few criticisms were aimed at the sound system and too much feedback from Lance's guitar, criticisms with which January agreed. When the auditorium was almost empty, she went backstage. This time, the usher recognized her and scarcely glanced at her press pass, simply nodded her through.

January was glad she'd waited. It would be less crowded backstage; Lance would have had a chance to relax a little, settle down, decide what he wanted to do. She glanced at her watch. It was early, just after eleven. Passing by Rick, she gave him a friendly smile, determined to get along with him.

For a change, he grinned too. "Lance is in his dressing room," he said. "Go right on in." His smile broadened.

Surprised, January said, "Thanks."

"No problem." Rick chuckled.

Maybe Lance had talked to him, January thought. As she put her hand on Lance's dressing room door, another door across the corridor swung open. It was Teri.

"January," she said. "Wait."

January pushed the door open. "What?" she said to Teri, but Teri was looking past her, into the dressing room. January looked in.

Lance, shirtless, was seated in a chair. On his lap, arms twisted around him, was a girl with long platinum hair. Lance had his face buried in her shoulder. Slowly she turned and saw January.

"Hi," the girl said, not moving. Her short black skirt was high on her thighs. The black silk top revealed more than it concealed. "I thing we've met before—in L.A., at Lance's. I'm Kim. Remember?"

Stunned, unable to move or speak, January nodded. She felt, she thought, like a butterfly must when it has been chloroformed and then impaled with a pin. Wanting to breathe; unable to. Wanting to get away; incapable of doing more than a slight wriggle.

Lance raised hes eyes to meet January's. Somehow, in self-defense she managed to take a step back.

"Thanks for taking such good care of Lance," said Kim. "He's been telling me *all* about you."

January's face went white. "How dare you?" she said.

"Wait," Lance said, "you don't understand."

"I understand everything," January said. She controlled her impulse to slam the door in his face. Somehow she managed to smile at Kim. "So glad you could make it," she said. "I was already growing tired of him." Quietly she closed the door on them, but not before she saw the anger blaze in Lance's green eyes.

Serves you right, she thought, walking rapidly down the hall, ignoring Rick's sardonic smile, Teri's voice calling her. She paid no attention as she heard Lance come running after her, yelling her name.

He caught up with her and grabbed her arm. "I told you to wait," he said.

"Take your hands off me," she said. "You don't have the right to tell me anything."

"Aren't you even going to let me explain?"

"Explain what?"

"About Kim."

January put her hands over her ears. "No," she said. "Don't bother. I don't want to hear it. That sort of explanation is a dime a dozen. I've heard it all before. I've heard some you'd never even dream of making up. Don't waste your breath. Save it for your shows."

Lance pulled her hands down from her ears. "Damn

you, January, I'm not Mike Stone. But I can't get you to believe that. Okay. No explanations. No excuses. You just believe what you damn well please." He turned away from her. As she headed for the door, he called after her, "You're a fool, January Warburton. You know that?"

She didn't pause, didn't turn to look back. Out on the street she leaned against the brick wall of the building and gave way briefly to tears. You sure are a fool, she told herself, a total fool. You fell for him. You knew what he was like but you fell for him anyway. The same as you did for Mike. For a full five minutes she leaned against the wall, sobbing. Then she took a deep breath, and straightened her shoulders.

From now on it would be strictly business. She had a job to do and she'd do it. After that, she'd never have to see Lance Devlin again in her entire life.

TOUR buses were like yachts, January mused as she stowed her duffel bag with the band's bags and clothes. The wide storage compartment clicked shut like the sure-catch on a ship's locker. Nothing was going to go bouncing out of there no matter how rough the voyage! All the furniture—card and eating tables, chairs, lamps—were stanchioned to the floor. There was a small galley and an even smaller bathroom—no, January thought, "head" in boat lingo. Small or not, though, everything they needed for their short voyage was in the tour bus. A utilitarian yacht—not a luxurious one by any means.

"We gotta name it," said Samson from the bunk where he was lounging. "Every good bus has a name."

Derek was seated in a chair, feet propped on a bunk rail. Teri was examining the contents of a small refrigerator.

"TV dinners," she listed, "grape juice, Coke, cream cheese, and spiced herring." She made a face and checked the overhead cupboard. "Crackers, crackers, and more crackers! Who stocked this place anyway?"

Rick clambered aboard. "I did." He had a bag in his arms. "And here's peanut butter, tuna fish, coffee, and beer. Okay?"

Teri shrugged. "Okay, but you're eating all that herring."

Joel, curled up on one of the other bunks, yawned and stretched. "Hey, guys, it's only six in the morning, how about some sleep?"

January peeked through the curtains drawn over the windows next to her. The nation's capital was still slumbering in the early dawn, the sky silver gray tinged with pink. The parking lot was practically empty. Stationed beside their bus was a second smaller one—the crew bus, loaded with equipment.

"Mutt and Jeff," she murmured.

"What did you say?" Teri asked.

"Mutt and Jeff," she repeated. "The buses look like Mutt and Jeff."

"Hey, everybody," Teri called out. "Guess what? January just named the buses."

"Now all we have to do is teach her to play guitar and she can join the group," said Samson.

"I'll teach her," said Derek.

Joel laughed. "Bet you will, too."

The wise remarks continued to fly between the three men. January sighed. They weren't really funny, but they tried. It was so typical of a tour—the strain, the early morning departure, the prospect of being cooped up on the bus for so many hours. Teri slid into the seat next to hers.

She glanced at her watch. "Where's Lance? I thought he wanted to be on the road in ten minutes." She was determined to be cool about Lance, talk casually and keep her feeling hidden.

"Didn't you know?" said Teri quickly. "Kim rented a car. They're driving to Philly together."

"Good," said January quickly—and meant it! The bus might be well equipped with armchairs, bunks, tables, a microwave oven, and a television, set up for playing films on cassettes, but it was too close, too intimate an atmosphere. She had dreaded, all last night, the idea of being in such a small space with Kim and Lance. And yesterday Kim had made it very clear she'd be on the road with them for a while—at least through Philadelphia, possibly as far as New Haven. She had to return to L.A., but she'd be back in time for the big New York concert. All this had come out in a group meeting yesterday afternoon during which details of the tour had been further discussed.

They had met in the hotel room designated as the hospitality room, a room set up for the band to meet with each other, meet the press and visitors—a general lounge for their use. In each hotel they stayed in, a room would be set aside for this purpose. Through the whole meeting, Kim, in a pair of jeans so tight that January wondered how she zipped them up, sat close to Lance. The T-shirt she wore clearly outlined her small breasts and pert little nipples. Her long silvery hair glistened even in the poor light from oversized lamps. She was beautiful, January had to admit to herself—she couldn't blame Lance for liking her.

During the meeting, Lance said very little, announcing only that as they had the first night off in Philly he wanted a rehearsal. He didn't like the way they were sounding on a couple of numbers. The band groaned, but agreed.

"I don't want to hear any complaints," Lance said. "In less than three weeks we're going to be playing Madison Square Garden. That's *the* arena, folks, the biggest. And we're going to be playing with some of the best groups in the country. We've got to be better than perfect."

"You got it," Teri said.

"You're always perfect," Kim said, slithering her body up his, folding her arms around his neck, and kissing him on the mouth.

"In your eyes only," Lance said, sliding a hand down her rib cage and then gently pushing her away. His eyes met January's. "Some people," he said, "consider me far less than perfect."

January met his look with a stony gaze, unflinchingly.

"Then some people," Kim said, glancing over at January, "are fools."

"That's what I say," Lance said with a smile, and bending his head gave Kim a kiss.

"Break it up, you idiots," Samson said. "We've got work to do. Let's have a little professionalism, Devlin."

The meeting broke up shortly afterward. Teri tried to catch January to talk to her, but January, pretending she hadn't heard her, hurried to her room. Damn him, she thought, feeling angry, frustrated, and humiliated all at once. And then, the hell with him, she thought right after, and dragged out her typewriter. Her fingers pounded the keys in a fury as she let out all her rage and hurt on paper. It was a habit of hers to write out what she was feeling, especially when there was no one she could really open up with and talk to. She knew Teri would listen, but Teri was in the band. Her loyalty to Lance came first. January thought it better to keep quiet and not cause any friction. Teri had even knocked on the door when she was writing, but January had explained she was busy typing up an article.

"You sure you don't want to talk?" Teri asked.

"What about?" January had answered.

"Okay," Teri had said, "if that's the way you want it."

Now, as she and Teri sat side by side on the bus, January was glad she hadn't said anything. She'd vented her feelings on the typewriter and then tore up the pages and thrown them away.

Lance wasn't here. She wasn't going to be tormented by his presence . . . with Kim at his side. She hated the jealousy that seeing him with another woman aroused in her. It was like an icy hand gripping her, altogether too reminiscent of the days with Mike. But different. Even more painful. The icy hand held a knife and twisted it in her stomach.

That beautiful day with Lance! She winced. The gallery, the food, the fun... culminating in the most exquisite lovemaking she'd ever known. Tears stung her eyes. She couldn't stand the thought that the day for Lance had been a way to kill time, to avoid thinking about the concert and his career. She blinked rapidly to keep the tears from forming and rolling down her cheeks. The worst of all was that for Lance their lovemaking could have been mere sex instead of the profound, deeply meaningful sharing it had been for her.

If that press agent, Diane, was right... January clenched her teeth. If Lance was going for the good reviews... she smiled bitterly. In this case "wooing the press" had to be the worst pun she'd ever heard. She took a deep breath and squared her shoulders. Now she would have to see to it that she didn't let her feelings get in the way again. There was a temptation to write scathingly cruel articles. But she knew she could never let herself do it. And she had to protect herself.

"Head 'em up. Roll 'em out," Rick's voice cracked out. The two buses started up and pulled out of the parking lot, the crew bus following the band's bus.

It was a rare privilege as a reporter to be allowed to tour with a band, but she had gained a reputation as an easy traveler and a good journalist. *Offbeat*'s readers were always clamoring for more of January's on-the-road stories. Through the articles, they felt they too were actually living with the rock group, traveling on the bus, playing the concerts, going backstage after a show. It gave them a vicarious thrill that they cherished. Past issues of January's on-the-road stories were always in demand.

And it was a strange feeling, January thought: wheels spinning down the highways, the bus their moving home, while beyond them all was stationary. Inside houses, as the band traveled from city to city, people were getting up, watering their gardens, sending their kids off to school, going to work. In here, as the morning wore on, Derek and Samson were playing gin rummy; Joel was watching Marx Brothers movies; Teri was knitting a sweater. When they stopped for breakfast, it was odd to see the people in the booths and at the counter, working people who came to this restaurant every day, and to realize that they, the travelers, might never be back here again. A few days on the road, January knew, and one began to feel like a gypsy, a nomad. One could spend weeks crisscrossing the country, north, south, east, west, playing here and there, a caravan on wheels, never staying long enough in one place to know people beyond chance meetings. Atmosphere and ambiance were sensed and lost in a matter of minutes.

It was no wonder, she thought, what happened to musicians after enough of going to a place, putting out all that energy, and then leaving again. She knew the things they did, the crazy things—not just the one-night stands, or even the use of drugs, often simply to stay awake and keep going—but the clothes-buying sprees, the collecting of odd paraphernalia, pins, buttons, etc. January thought it made them feel that they'd actually touched a place. Otherwise the sense of time going too fast and experience missed was too deeply troubling.

She remembered one rock group that was making a fortune. The lead guitarist bought a new guitar in every city they hit. Not even good guitars or ones he ever played; but he bought them and scribbled on them the name of the place in which he'd bought them, "so," he said, "as to be sure that I'd really been there and not just dreamed it all." Because after a while it did all begin to feel like a dream, a dream in constant motion.

Despite having stopped for a leisurely breakfast, they made good time and were checked into their hotel rooms by ten-thirty.

"I don't see what the point was of getting up so early.

We could still be asleep right now," Joel griped.

"Because I want a rehearsal this afternoon," Lance said. He had gotten there ahead of them and met them in the lobby. Kim was nowhere to be seen.

"You can rest now," Lance said, "get some lunch, and meet me over at the auditorium this afternoon at two sharp. No one's to be late. You've got tonight off to get a lot of rest because we're doing those double shows for the next three days—matinee and evening. By the way, I don't know if Rick told you, but we have an opening act here in Philly, a local group."

Lance paused and looked around as if to be sure all his various messages had sunk in. "Okay. I'll see you this afternoon. The hospitality room's number three-oh-four and there's a press party at six, a sort of welcome to Philly, so everyone be there."

The band members, keys in hand, headed for the elevators and their rooms. Joel and Teri of course shared a room. Derek and Samson doubled up also. Lance was the only one with a room of his own.

"I want to speak to you," he said sharply to January as she started for the elevator. "What's your room number?"

She turned to face him. "Speak to me here."

"In private. I want to talk to you in private."

"This is private enough," she said, indicating the lobby which was almost empty.

At that moment, two girls who appeared to be in their early teens came up to Lance. They had his albums in hand and were giggling with embarrassment.

"You're Lance Devlin, aren't you?" said one.

The other nudged her. "Of course he is. Look at him."

Lance was smiling, but holding on to January's arm.

"Sign this," said the first girl, "please."

Lance grinned. He spun January around, took the pen held out to him, and asked, "What's your name?"

"Missy."

"You don't mind being my desk I hope," he whispered in January's ear.

His warm breath feathered her hair, sent a tremulous shudder along her spine. She ground her teeth. "How can I mind," she hissed. "You've got me in a hammerlock hold."

He chuckled and signed the album cover. "How come you're not in school, Missy?" He took the other girl's album.

Missy shrugged. "We knew you'd be here. We checked. My Dad works for the papers. He had your itinerary. He's going to be at your press thing tonight but he wouldn't bring me, so we ducked school and came over." She was talking very fast, practically tripping over words.

"What's your Dad's name? I'll look for him this evening."

"Walters," said Missy, "Jack Walters. Only don't tell him I was here, okay, 'cause he'd kill me."

"You better get to school," said Lance. "Coming to the show tomorrow?"

Missy nodded. "Both of us are."

"Okay," said Lance. "I'll send out a song to you. Got a request?"

"'Diamonds of the Sea.'"

"Sorry," Lance said. He turned January toward him and wrapped her in his arms so her body was pressed close against his. "That song is taken," he said hoarsely, his eyes staring deep into hers. "It's taken for all time." Then, with apparent difficulty, Lance broke their gaze, but he pulled away only slightly, just enough to face the girls and tell them firmly to get off to school. He was smiling as they skipped out the front door, clutching their albums and waving goodbye to him. Awed, exultant expressions covered their young faces.

January felt a curious mixture of emotions, not the least of which was bitterness at Lance's power over females young and old.

"Okay," he said, "let's go," pulling her toward the elevator.

"Take your hands off me," she said angrily. "I said we could talk here."

"And I said," Lance said, releasing her arm as the elevator doors closed behind them, "I wanted to talk in private. That lobby is not private. What floor are you on?"

"My duffel bag's down in the lobby."

"Fine. I'll send someone up with it. What floor are you on?"

"None of your business."

"Okay." He pushed 4. "We'll go to my room."

"Kim'll love that, I'm sure."

"She won't care. Anyway, she's not there. She went shopping."

"Why?" snapped January. "She doesn't have any clothes tight enough?"

"Jealous?" said Lance softly.

The elevator came to a halt. Immediately January pushed the button for the lobby.

"What are you doing?" said Lance.

"Going down to get my bag. Do you want to get off here?"

"I don't believe this. No, I'll go down with you."

"Fine."

In the lobby January grabbed her bag and got back in the elevator where Lance was waiting, holding the door for her. She pushed 3. "We can go to the hospitality room," she said.

"There'll be people in there setting up for the press party."

"Too bad."

Lance suddenly snatched January's key out of her hand. He studied the number and then her face. "Three-oh-seven. Good. At least we're going to the right floor."

"Give me my key back," she demanded.

The elevator stopped. "We get out here, I believe."

"My key," January said furiously.

Lance opened the door to her room, took her duffel

bag from her, and threw it down on the bed. He caught her shoulders in his hands. "Haven't you had enough?"

"Haven't you?" she retorted. As angry as she was, his hands on her body were having their own effect. She stepped back from him. "You said you wanted to talk to me. Talk."

"I want to tell you about Kim."

"I don't want to hear about Kim."

"Well, listen anyway." He took a step toward her and she backed away more. "January, what are you so scared of?"

"I don't want you touching me."

He was instantly apologetic. "I'm sorry. Did I hurt you? I didn't mean to."

"No," she said, her voice breaking, "you didn't hurt me. Just leave me alone, please."

"No," he said. "I can't. I don't want to."

"Then what do you want?" She had backed against the wall and was leaning there, suddenly feeling tired, defenseless. Whatever it was he had to say, she wished now he'd say it and get it over with. She didn't want to fight with him anymore.

She didn't move as he walked up to her, put his arms on either side of her, hands against the wall behind her. She waited, not feeling trapped as she knew she ought to. She leaned her head back and closed her eyes. "Go ahead," she said. "Talk."

"There's only one way to communicate with you right now," he said throatily. And, instead of hearing words, she felt his lips against hers, his body pressing her body against the wall. She felt suddenly weak, and began to tremble as his hands moved from the nape of her neck around to the smooth skin of her throat, slowly down over her body. As insistent as his body was, pinning her back against the wall, his lips were gentle, teasing, so that she found herself reaching up, her hands burying themselves in his hair as she tried to draw his mouth closer.

His hands were on the zipper that ran down the length

of the jumpsuit. Underneath it, she wore nothing but a pair of tiny lace bikini underpants. He drew the zipper down halfway, parting the material. His lips moved down the side of her throat. His hands went inside the jumpsuit, reaching upward to stroke her breasts. His touch was so gentle. Oh, very sexy and arousing, but so gentle. And his terribly, terribly tender touch was expressing love, January just knew it. Those fingertips that created intense emotion in his music were telling her as much about his passion for her body as about his caring for her, the emotional, intelligent human being, January Warburton. Her body felt like it was sliding down the wall, closer into his. All thought of resisting him for any reason at all was a shadow in the back of her brain. Her body was crying yes, almost begging for all of him. When his mouth found her breasts, his tongue teasing her nipples into points of fire and his hands sliding lower down over her hips, slowly inward, she could only arch her back, wanting to give as much to him as he was giving to her.

In a single easy motion, he swept her up in his arms, murmuring her name softly. He carried her to the bed and laid her down gently, unzipping the jumpsuit the rest of the way. His lean body was pressed against hers, fingers tracing dizzying circles over the lace of her panties. At last he slid them off and his pelvis began to move in a provocative rhythm. They were rising to dizzying heights, making ecstatic love to each other, fulfilling and being fulfilled.

They lay entwined and January was overwhelmed by a blissful contentment that surpassed anything she'd known before.

"You know there aren't words for what's happened between us, don't you?" Lance murmured, stroking her hip.

January couldn't speak. She could only nod.

Lance began to hum. It was a new tune, one January knew she'd never heard, yet a melody so hauntingly lovely it moved her deeply—profoundly. She drifted, listening to Lance, knowing they didn't have to talk now.

There was a lifetime ahead for thrashing out misunderstandings.

And then the phone rang. The harsh, overloud sound—so unwelcome, so unexpected—made January's body start. She grabbed the receiver.

"January," came Kim's high, sweet voice, "is Lance with you?"

There was a sudden, enormous lump in January's throat and her voice faltered. "Yes—s. Yes, he is."

"Oh, thank heaven," Kim said. "Please tell him I need him. I really need him. Now. Tell him just that, will you, January?"

She didn't reply. Slowly she replaced the receiver on the cradle and repeated Kim's exact words. She was somewhat stunned, a bit frightened too.

She was even more deeply frightened by Lance's reaction. Like a lightning flash he was on his feet, scrambling into his clothes.

"Got to go to her, hon," he said matter-of-factly before giving January a peck on the cheek.

"Obviously," she drawled sarcastically. But Lance missed the unpleasantness of her reaction; he was out, the door clicking shut behind him even as the word echoed in the room.

January sat alone on the large, rumpled bed . . . her fragile but exquisite happiness shattered.

chapter

9

LANCE didn't call—not after rehearsal, not before the show. There was just a short note in her box after dinner.

"Trust me, love, this is important."

And January tried. But when she saw Lance backstage after the concert, Kim wound around his arm and gazing starry-eyed at him, it was simply too much! Hurt and jealous, January stormed out of the dressing room. He was on her heels and grabbed her at the stage door.

"What's the matter with you?" Lance demanded.

"Matter?" she screeched. "That's the most absurd question I've ever heard. What do you *think* is the matter?"

"Kim," he said flatly.

"Damned right!"

His eyes narrowed as he studied her. "January," he

said at last, "I know you're vulnerable and insecure. Aren't we all? But this is ridiculous. You can't trust me because you can't trust yourself. Why not go with your feelings about me?"

She was speechless and he rushed on. "Kim's an old friend. And she's got a problem that right now only I can help her with. Won't you support me, stand by me on this one?"

"While you cozy up to another woman?" Instantly January regretted that catty question.

Lance had gone rigid. Fires danced in his eyes and a muscle twitched in his jaw. "Trust, loyalty—maybe call it devotion—whatever, I need it. Especially from you." He seemed very tired suddenly. "Can you give, January, really give, or only take?"

She drew in her breath on a sharp pain. The question was an insult. Or a barb that cut to the quick.

"I . . . I need space, Lance, space and time to answer that."

For several days, January didn't see Lance at all, except at press parties and concerts. They avoided one another. He seemed to be with Kim every time January caught sight of him. When they left Philadelphia for New Haven, January rode on the bus; Lance and Kim drove. So far the shows were going extremely well, except for two numbers which continued to be weak.

The first night in Philadelphia, Lance had introduced "Diamonds" with the remark, "For someone out there who isn't sure whether she loves me or hates me." January did not respond or even acknowledge the remark later. But he continued to dedicate the song to her at every show, sometimes cracking the band up with his introductions. Once he said, "Will the person to whom this song is dedicated please stand up?" January didn't move. Another time he said, "To the reporter whom I have every reason to loathe but instead love," which caused more than one head to turn. Offstage he never spoke to her. Nor did Kim, though a couple of times she seemed on the verge of it.

January's emotions were in turmoil and she wished desperately that everyone would leave her alone. Even Adrian, when she called to check in and give information, asked all sorts of leading questions and said that he'd heard rumors that Lance was continually dedicating a song to her. January wanted to hang up the phone in disgust.

In New Haven, January dragged out the typewriter and sat down to write an article. Adrian was waiting for a story. Writing about Lance was easier than she had anticipated. She was able to maintain objectivity, praising most of the shows, criticizing the numbers that the band already knew were weak. She described audience reactions and the general atmosphere on the road. Her closing line said that at every show Lance was dedicating the song "Diamonds of the Sea" to a mysterious woman who never showed herself. She suggested that maybe the woman was a figment of Lance's imagination. That'll stop the rumors, she thought.

"It'll do," Adrian said about the article the next day on the phone, "but you've written better. There's something lacking. I can't pinpoint what it is—a certain oomph."

"Maybe it's just on-the-road fatigue," she answered.

"Maybe," said Adrian. "So write about that then. Is the whole band afflicted, or just you? By the way, you don't mention Lance enough. I mean, you have him onstage and at the press parties—public situations—but where's the private stuff? That's what you're on the road with them for, to get the behind-the-scenes dope on Lance. You haven't got any of that in here."

"I don't see him that much," explained January. "He's never around. He's not traveling on the bus. He's always in his car with his girlfriend."

"Well, get more of her in here, then," said Adrian. "Anyway, if he had a girlfriend, how come he's dedicating all those songs to someone else? Come on, January, there's something here you're not telling and your readers are going to know it. They want Lance Devlin. He's the star, and from what we're hearing back here, he's growing bigger every day. Both *Time* and *Newsweek* mentioned him last week. He's climbing right up there with Bruce Springsteen and Tom Petty. Platinum is speeding up the record release so as to have it out the same day as the Madison Square Garden show. That means, the same day of his biggest show, his album comes out. By the time, he gets back to L.A., they're going to be crazy here. You've got to get more stuff on him."

"I don't see him that much."

"See him more," commanded Adrian. "That's your job, January. I want an interview with him. An exclusive. No one gets interviews with Lance Devlin. Even you haven't given us one yet. You get one and we'll feature it—build the whole next issue around Lance and L.A. Expressway. Get his girlfriend in it if you have to. What's her name?"

January sighed. "Kim." She didn't like the idea of having to pin Lance down for an interview. It would mean having to spend hours with him.

Adrian interrupted her thoughts. "Kim Chiles? Is that the one?"

"That's the one," said January, trying to sound non-chalant.

"Are you sure she's his girlfriend?" said Adrian. "I know her. I always thought..."

"They drive a car together," January cut in, "they share a room together. They eat, sleep, drink, talk, walk together. I don't know what else you'd call it."

Adrian laughed. "Green-eyed jealousy rearing its ugly head, January?"

"No," she snapped.

"Well if not," said Adrian easily, "then one must assume you are all good friends, getting along just fine. So in that case, why don't you see if you can't get into that car with them. Take a day off from the bus. I want Lance, January. The hell with the band—they're good, but they're not the main attraction. He is. Get him. I want morning, noon, and night with Lance Devlin."

January sighed. "Okay, Adrian. You'll get your story." She hung up.

And called Lance. Quickly. Before she lost her nerve.

"Hi," she said, trying to sound casual. "I have to speak to you. It's January."

Lance's voice was cautious. "What's up?"

"I just talked to Adrian. He's not satisfied with my last story. He says there's too much about the band and not enough about you. He wants an interview."

Lance was hesitant. "With me?"

"Yes," said January, "and that's not all." She paused, hating what she was going to have to ask for. "He says he has enough of the band in the bus. He says if you're riding separately in a car, then he wants me to go along in the car with you."

Lance began to laugh. "He does, does he? He wants you to ride in the car with me and Kim?"

"It's not funny," said January.

'I think it's very funny," said Lance. "We have only one problem."

"What's that?" asked January.

"Kim's leaving tomorrow."

January tried to quell the sudden pang of excitement she felt surge through her. Forget it, she told herself. "I see. Does that mean you'll be riding on the bus, then?"

"No," said Lance. "It means that you and I will be riding in the car together."

"No way," said January quickly.

"You want your interview, don't you?"

"Yes, but..."

"If you want your interview, you'll get it in the car on the way from New Haven to Providence. Anything else Adrian wants?"

"Behind-the-scenes stuff," January answered. "More about you. Morning, noon, and night with Lance Devlin was what he said."

"Really?" Lance's voice became softly insinuating.

"That's easily provided. You can have all the morning, noon, and night you want."

January tried to ignore the conflict of emotions within her which ranged from sweet aching desire to seething rage at both Adrian and Lance for putting her in this position. "Backstage before a concert would be fine," she said primly. "More than enough. And if I could hang around for a day or something—sort of observe your life."

Lance chuckled. "Remember what happens when we hang around together?"

"I remember," said January.

"You think the same thing wouldn't happen all over again if we spent a day together? January, about this space you need, what I said . . ."

"Nothing's going to happen," she said sharply. "I have to get a story, Lance Devlin, because if I don't, I could lose my job."

"Lose your job? That's crazy. You're Adrian's star reporter."

"I know, but . . ."

"Okay, January," Lance said. "You'll get your story. Business only, right now. Isn't that what you want? We'll play it your way."

"Thanks," January said. When she hung up she realized her hand was shaking. Kim was leaving. What if Kim had never arrived on the scene at all? She dismissed the idea. There were certain things she didn't dare think about.

The next three days seemed both to rocket by and to drag on interminably. The New Haven Coliseum, where the band was playing, was filled to capacity every night. People were coming from New York and all over Connecticut to see Lance and L. A. Expressway. The show was getting better at each performance: Lance and Teri cruising through the songs with unbelievable ease and harmony. Samson twirled his drumsticks in the air like a cheerleader's batons, tossing them up with a flourish, catching them with a flick of the wrist, and coming in right on the beat. Joel drew rounds of exuberant applause for his fluid improvisations on the keyboards; and Derek, steady, understated, seemed to be the quiet strength of the group.

But it was Lance who had the concert-goers on their feet, Lance who had girls screaming, jumping up from their seats, swooning in the aisles. In his tight-fitting pants, his shirts open to the waist, his golden-brown hair curling over his collar, he was riveting. When he cupped the microphone in one hand, letting his guitar hang at his side, tilted his body forward, and made his voice go low and husky, every female felt he was singing only to her. They all had fantasies of being alone with him for just one night. And when his hand slammed down on the guitar, his fingers digging into the strings, making it wail and moan, they all went into ectasy, the sound seeming to rip and tear through their bodies. Yet he was the gentle lover too, with his voice reaching out to caress, touch, fondle. His energy was boundless and he gave his all.

The second night in New Haven he did a slow ballad for his last number. Like the rest of the audience, January was mesmerized. Watching Lance bathed in the soft blue haze of the lights, she knew she was experiencing the work of a true artist. As his voice faded away at the end of the song, there was a total breathless silence for several seconds before the audience went wild.

January watched it all in amazement, as she watched every show. She was accustomed to seeing bands get lazy or laid back the longer they were on the road. Not so with Lance. Every night he made sure that each show was better than the last. And in each show, as the lights played over his body, he became to January more and more irresistible.

She had hoped, gradually, his appeal would wear off, that she would no longer want him, but see him as one more musician: attractive, talented—and desired by too many women for his own good . . . or hers. Mike's un- faithfulness haunted her. And Kim haunted her. Yet she wanted Lance, until sometimes it was a tangible, physical ache. She felt foolish. She was weak-kneed around Lance, nervous, edgy, jittery. And her only concern was that no one, most especially he, should know. So she tried her very best to act poised, cool, calm. But as the day they were due to drive to Providence together grew closer, she found it harder and harder to keep up the image. Inside she was a wreck. She was so crazy in love with him, so uncertain of him and herself. In the intimacy of being several hours in a car together, Lance was sure to see how she felt.

Finally the day came.

"Hope you don't mind giving up the luxuries of the bus," said Lance as they settled into the car. He slid open the sun roof and rolled down the windows to let the soft New England light in.

"It's kind of a relief," January admitted. "We've watched every film five hundred times, read all the books, played every card game, and sung every song. It's reached a point now where all we do is lie around on the bunks playing idiotic word games. Teri's on her second sweater and Samson has taken to reading comic books like a fiend. We're going nuts."

Lance laughed. "Yeah, I know how it gets." He started the car.

January found herself staring at his hands, his long, slender fingers holding the wheel easily. He was in his usual faded jeans and black T-shirt. Despite all her jitters, she felt comfortable, glad to be with him, almost as if he were an old friend.

He glanced over at her, green eyes soft. "I've missed you," he said. "For two people on tour together we don't see much of each other."

January was silent, uncertain of what to say.

"How are you with maps?" Lance asked. He reached into the glove compartment, pulled one out, and handed it to her. "I thought we might take it slow. Take the scenic route. There's no show till tomorrow."

She spread the map out on her lap and his finger traced the roads.

"We see the water if we go along this way. Supposedly it's really pretty. I haven't had a chance to see anything so far, and I love New England. I thought before going to Providence we might stop off in Newport. I've always wanted to spend some time in that town." He laughed. "Sentimental. All the great jazz and folk festivals used to be there. And I hear they've got some terrific restaurants. What do you say?"

"That'd be nice," January said. Her voice sounded stiff, stilted to her ears.

"We don't have to," Lance said quickly. "I know how you feel about me. You can't trust me. And I can't stand lack of trust. We can just drive straight through, do the interview. It's only that," he hesitated, "I could use a break. I'm tired. This past week's been rough, really rough. I don't feel I've had much time to relax."

Not even with Kim, January wanted to throw at him, but didn't.

"Couldn't we try to be friends?" she asked instead.

"Is that the way you really want it?" asked Lance.

"Isn't it the best way?"

"Okay," said Lance, "we'll try." He held out his hand to her. "Shake on it."

But as they clasped hands and his eyes met hers, lingering a second too long, January knew somewhere deep inside that no matter what she said, she could never even pretend at mere friendship with Lance.

"Come on, reporter," he said with a smile. "Get your tape recorder out."

As she asked standard questions and he answered, they drove through a series of small towns. Lilac and forsythia were in bloom, hazy lavender and rich yellow. They passed clapboard houses, picket fences, and old wooden churches. Dark green shutters were open to let the spring air in; roses turned outward to the sun. Small sailboats darted through the sparkling blue Atlantic waters. January and Lance found themselves interrupting their interview often to point out something to one another—a piece of architecture, a brilliant garden, or simply the smell of the sea, the feel of the breeze. At one point, for the fun of it, they veered off the main road, taking a side street that wound through the New England countryside. Stone walls and elms, maples, and birches lined the road.

"This is great," Lance said. "I finally feel like I'm getting a day off. This is exactly what I wanted to do all along—drive, see the scenery, relax." He stopped the car. "You want to get out here?" They were beside a large, open meadow.

"Do you think it's okay?" January said. "It's not private property?"

"There's no one around. Come on." He got out, went around to the other side of the car, and opened the door for her. January was touched by the unexpected Old World gesture.

He took her hand as he helped her out of the car, but then let it go immediately.

They climbed over the stone wall onto the field. The grass was dry and matted but interspersed with the light green of new growth. Red, yellow, and orange wildflowers added little dabs of color. January spread her arms, took a deep breath, and spun herself around. "It's beautiful," she said exultantly. "We had a field like this when I was a little girl, up in Santa Barbara where I lived. My mother still lives there. My favorite thing in the whole world was to lie down in the field and roll in the grass, over and over."

"Do it," said Lance.

She looked at him hesitantly and then began to laugh. "Why not?" She threw herself down onto the earth and began to roll, finally sitting up, eyes filled with laughter, hair tumbling about her shoulders. Lance came over and knelt down beside her, gently plucking bits of dry grass out of her hair.

"I must look ridiculous," she said.

"No," he replied. "You don't. You look very lovely."

At that moment, January realized that all she wanted was for Lance to take her in his arms and kiss her.

He didn't. He stood up, shoved his hands deep in his pockets, and walked away from her. His back turned to her, he said, "I suppose we ought to get going."

January stood up, more disappointed than she cared to admit to herself, and brushed herself off. In silence they walked to the car. He didn't look at her as he held the door for her. Without a word to her, he drove back to the main road.

"Lance," she said tentatively after a while, "are you angry?"

"Huh?" he said, as if startled out of private thoughts. "No, I'm not angry. Sorry, I didn't mean to seem that way. I was thinking about something. Is the interview over? Was there anything else you wanted to ask?"

January shook her head. "I got enough," she said.

"Check the map. Where's the turnoff to Newport?"

"Then you still want to go?" January said, suddenly relieved. She'd been afraid he'd changed his mind.

"Sure, don't you?"

"Definitely."

"Great. There's a little restaurant where they supposedly have the best clam chowder in the world. I thought we could go there for lunch."

But Lance seemed distant. Even as they ate delicious chowder in Newport's famous Black Pearl Restaurant and later walked along the waterfront admiring the renovated buildings and the graceful yachts, January sensed a coolness. It was like the hostility she'd felt when they first met. He wasn't rude or flippant. He was in fact more genial, more open than he'd never been with her, and yet she sensed a deep guardedness. She wished he'd take her hand, even flirt with her, tease her as he'd done in the past, but he didn't. He was being, she realized, a friend, nothing more and nothing less. He wasn't going to make any more passes at her; he was going to respect her wishes; and she found herself bitterly regretting her confusion, deeply unhappy that she'd ever said anything about being just friends.

You can't have it all, Warburton, she told herself. She was afraid that if they became lovers, he wouldn't be capable of being faithful, and she knew it would destroy her if he weren't. But if they didn't become lovers, then there would be no more of that giddy, dizzying sensation, no more joy, no more exhilaration. And no more turmoil and upheaval and confusion, she reminded herself—no more anger, no more pain. She sighed.

"Tired?" Lance asked.

"Oh no," she said, and then added, "well a little, maybe."

"Let's go back to the car," he said. "We ought to get going anyway."

It occurred to January that as there was no show that night, they could have stayed in Newport—gone to an inn, taken a room, slept together.... She tried to steer her thoughts in another direction but they refused to go. She found herself imagining what a whole night with Lance would be like, remembering the days together. A night, an entire night with him.... Her lips parted as she thought of it.

"What are you thinking about?" said Lance, seeing the expression on her face.

She started. "Huh? What? Oh, nothing." She blushed.

He stared at her. "Nothing? Why are you turning so red?"

She turned her face away, but he caught her chin with his hand and made her face him. "What?" he repeated.

"Nothing," she said, trying to duck her head. "Please, Lance."

He let her go abruptly. "It didn't look like nothing to me," he said curtly.

The ride to Providence was silent, both of them lost in their own thoughts. January berated herself. Why hadn't she taken what he offered? She should have let herself go ahead and have a fling with him, even if it wasn't going to last, even if it meant hurt and heartache in the end. A few nights of happiness, a week, a month—it would have been better than what she'd had for the past year and a half.

She thought of Mike and knew she was kidding herself. She wasn't that type of person. A year, a month, a week—it wasn't good enough for her. She wanted a lasting relationship, one which was mutually sustaining and supportive; one in which the partners took care of each other, helped one another; what she had thought she would have with Mike. They could have their separate careers—that was fine. But when it came to the rest of it, she wanted an exclusive relationship. No Kim, no Susie or Beckie or Marilyn or whoever; the two of them, to have and to hold, for better or worse. She smiled to herself. Despite her experiences on the road, and all her time on the music scene, she was still an old-fashioned woman.

Lance caught the smile playing on her lips. "What?" he said, uttering his first word since they'd left Newport.

"Laughing at myself, I guess."

"About anything particular?"

"Not really. Only that I guess I'm as traditional and conservative as I've often suspected I am."

"There's nothing wrong with that."

"Maybe not, but it's not too fashionable these days."

"Fashion's not important," Lance said.

"How could you of all people say that?" January said. "You make your living from fashion."

"Fads perhaps. What's in. But that doesn't mean I take it seriously."

"What do you take seriously?" January asked abruptly.

"My music."

"You just said..."

"I don't consider most of the music I play as *my* music. Some of the songs, yes, such as 'Diamonds of the Sea.'" He glanced at her as if to demand some recognition for all the times he'd dedicated the song to her. She said nothing. "A few others," he went on, "but most of the music I do right now is for the money, to get established."

"You're succeeding at that," she said.

"Yes, but it's not enough," Lance said. "It's teenage stuff. Everybody in the band—Teri, Joel, Samson, Derek—they're all much better musicians than most people would realize. They all have classical training, and they know everything else as well—jazz, folk, blues. We all do. And we haven't begun to tap what we're capable of. That'll come, though, in time. It's a matter of being taken seriously—by the people in the music business, and by our audiences.

"I could have started right into classical. I had the background. But if I'd done that, they'd have never stopped comparing me with my parents. I had to start at the other end of the spectrum and come around. We're trying now to develop a sound which is ours, uniquely ours, like no one else's. The Stones did that, the Beatles, the Who. All the great groups. Especially the Beatles— not only did they have their own sound, but they took pop music way beyond where it's ever been before. That's what I want to do."

January was listening quietly. Lance had never opened up so fully on the subject of his music before.

"May I use any of that," she asked, "in my interview? Would you mind?"

He shrugged. "Sure, go ahead. I don't care."

They had come into Providence while they were talking. Lance pulled the car up in front of a gray stone building.

"This is it," he said. "Our latest residence." He glanced up at the hotel. "Not bad, I guess."

He helped January get her duffel bag out of the trunk. "Check in time," he said. "Got everything?"

She nodded.

They signed in together at the desk and then took the elevator up to the fifth floor.

"Down the hall from each other again." Lance grinned. "See you later. Enjoy the show tonight." He walked away leaving her standing there, staring after him.

She went to her room, closed the door hard behind her, and sat down on the bed. Tears of frustration came to her eyes.

Well, she said to herself, that's over. He doesn't even like me anymore—if he ever did.

Dismayed with herself for her own inconsistency, she pulled out her typewriter and set it up, then turned on her tape recorder and began to play back the interview, transcribing it as she listened.

Writing up interviews from tapes was usually the easiest thing in the world for her, more like taking dictation than anything else, but this time it went badly. She kept losing track of what Lance had said and having to go back and replay. Gradually she realized that all she was doing was listening to the sound of his voice and paying no attention to what he was actually saying.

She snapped off the tape recorder and rested her head in her hands. I can't go on this way, she thought to herself. I have to do something. It's too ridiculous.

She stood up and paced the floor, a flurry of thoughts dashing through her head. She knew what she wanted to do. But could she? Did she dare?

"You don't have any choice, Warburton," she said aloud to her image in the mirror. Her hair was messy. There were still a few bits of grass in it. Her shirt was untucked and her jeans looked like they could stand a good washing. Life on the road, she thought to herself. She reached for her brush, began to pull it through her hair, and then abruptly dropped it.

The hell with it, she thought, and not even bothering to tuck in her shirt, she grabbed her key off the dresser, shoved it in her pocket, and strode out of her room, letting the door slam shut behind her. Lance's room was 528. She walked down to it, all too aware of what she was doing.

At his door, she knocked once.

He opened it almost immediately. "January," he said in surprise. "What do you want?"

She stood there for a second, blindly uncertain, and then took a deep breath. "You," she said, "I want you."

He looked at her, "What do you mean? You need more for the interview?"

For a minute she thought he was teasing her, making fun of her, and then gradually realized he wasn't; he really didn't understand what she wanted.

"No," she cried. "I mean I want you." Her voice was low, but she was certain now of what she was doing and what she was saying. "I want you, Lance. I want to go to bed with you. I want to love you."

He opened the door wider. "Come in," he said softly.

chapter

10

"SIT DOWN," said Lance.

January sat.

"I'm not going to do it," he said, facing her. "I'm not going to make love with you."

A startled look swept January's face. "Don't you want to?" she asked after a moment.

Lance shrugged. "Maybe, but I'm not going to."

January sat in total silence for a few moments, unable to tear her eyes away from Lance's. "I thought you wanted me," she finally said.

Lance turned away from her. "I thought you wanted to be friends," he said. "Nothing more."

"I do, or rather I did, but..."

"But now you want to have everything," said Lance. "Friends and lovers, is that it? It won't work, January,

131

it can't. You said yourself you're an old-fashioned woman."

"Yes, but I realized something." She drew herself up straighter. "Lance, please, look at me."

He turned toward her.

"I—it's more important to me to be able to have you whatever way I can. Today, when we were together, you were so respectful, but I missed your teasing. I missed the way you used to act with me. At first I thought we could be friends and it would work, everything would be okay. But I was wrong. I . . ." she lowered her eyes.

"You don't know what you want. "You see me on-stage, doing my thing. You remember our two times together. It was good. You want more. I don't blame you. It was good for me, too. But it's not enough, January. You don't even know me. You've got a schoolgirl crush, that's all. It's not me you want, January, it's the guy you see onstage. And you don't even trust that guy."

"What about you?" said January, suddenly angry. "What did you want? To seduce the reporter to keep her from writing nasty things about you? To prove you could make me want you? What was it you said ages ago? That I wanted you as much as you wanted me and that you were going to wait until I asked for you. Okay, I asked. Now are you happy?"

Before he could say a word, she leaped from the chair and dashed to the door. She was wrenching it open as he grabbed her arm and swung her around to face him.

"No, January," he said, "I'm not happy. You're right. I seduced you. Maybe I did want to prove something, but I don't anymore." His grip on her arm relaxed but he didn't let her go.

"Then what do you want?" she said. There were tears in her eyes; her lower lip was quivering. At any moment, she knew she was going to burst into tears.

"I want . . ." he reached up, caught a silky strand of hair in his fingers, stroked it gently back off her face.

One tear spilled over and then a second. He brushed

them away with his thumb. "I want you to stop crying," he said.

"I can't," she whispered.

"Let me help you," he said, putting his arms around her, drawing her close and holding her in a warm embrace. "I care about you, January," he said. "I don't want to hurt you."

The phone rang.

"Damn," he said, pulling back from her. "I have to answer it. It may be about the show."

She nodded, suddenly feeling enormously relieved. He cared about her. Lord, how much she'd wanted to hear that!

Lance picked up the phone by the table on the bed, eyes still on January. "Hello... Oh, hi... no, I thought it was about the band.... When?... Boston? Okay. How's everything back there?... No, just January.... Yeah, I'm trying.... Right, see you in a few days then. 'Bye." He hung up. "That was Kim," he said, watching January's expression.

She didn't move, said nothing.

"She's coming here in a few days."

Silent, January waited for whatever was coming next.

"She asked me if I'd explained things to you yet. I told her I was trying."

Lance walked over to her and took her hands in his. "Will you let me explain now? Will you listen?"

She nodded.

"Kim and I've known each other for years, ever since we were little kids. We grew up together. Her parents and mine were friends. Kim and her family stuck by us through that whole scandal when nobody else would. Kim and Teri—they were my best friends."

He paused. "Kim is, how should I put it, an actress. I mean she wants to be an actress, she wants to make her living that way, but she also is one by nature. She always has been. She can't help it. I remember when we were children—she was always playing one role after another." Lance laughed at the memory. "She could become any character she wanted. You've seen her do that."

January wasn't so sure she had.

"The one thing you've got to understand," said Lance, "is that I love Kim. I always have; I always will. No matter what she does, no matter how she behaves."

She'd known it all along but still, when she heard the words, when she heard him say he loved Kim, January felt like she was drowning. She felt she was sinking into a dark hole, cold, airless, and tight. Water was closing over her head and she could hardly hear what Lance was saying. Words about Kim's groupie act; something about her liking to annoy the press; something else about a pact they'd made. But most of it January didn't understand, couldn't hear, and when the door was flung open and Rick burst in, she could only feel relieved.

"Sound system, man," said Rick to Lance without even looking at January. "It's screwed up. Something's wrong. You gotta come down right away. If they don't work it out, we haven't got a show tomorrow. One of the amps sounds like hell. We may have to replace it."

Lance was already halfway out the door. He turned and said hurriedly to January, "We'll talk more later. There's a lot to it and I want you to understand, okay?"

She nodded, but she knew there was nothing more to be said. She'd heard all she needed to.

Slowly she walked down the corridor to her room. On her way she met Derek.

"Hi," he said. "Where are they off to?"

"Rick and Lance? Something wrong with the sound system. One of the amps."

"Yeah," said Derek. "I noticed that the other night. Weird sounds coming out of it. I thought maybe it was going to blow. I mentioned it to Tim, one of the roadies, but he probably never told Rick. I wonder if I ought to go over there. I feel like it was sort of my fault."

"It wasn't your fault," January said. "You told someone. If he didn't pass the word on, you're not to blame."

"Maybe, but I ought to have told Rick or Lance. That's the amp closest to me. The others can't hear it the way I do. I'm always standing right beside it."

"Well," January said, "if it'd make you feel better, go on over, but they probably already have about forty people working on it."

Derek's glum expression lifted. "Probably," he said, smiling. "So what are you doing? Pacing the hallways?"

January managed a grin. "Sort of. I was on my way to my room."

"Oh." Derek looked at her for a few seconds. "Are you, um, are you free tonight? I mean, we don't have a show tonight, and I've been meaning to ask you. I mean what I mean is . . ."

January suppressed a hysterical urge to laugh. She knew if he said "I mean" one more time she really *would* laugh.

"How about dinner tonight?"

January suddenly relaxed. "Sure, why not?" she said. It would be good for her to spend an evening with someone else; better than sitting around her hotel room moping and feeling sorry for herself.

"I don't mean with the whole band," Derek was saying. "Just me."

January touched his hand. "I know. I'd love to, really."

"Great," said Derek. "About seven-thirty? I'll meet you in the hospitality room."

"Perfect," said January. "See you later."

She watched him walk down the hall and wondered if going out with him was a fair thing to do. She was only doing it to take her mind off Lance for a while. She shrugged as she went into her room. So what, she thought. Everyone used everyone. That's the way things worked. And then she immediately regretted the thought. Derek was a nice guy; she liked him; she had no intention of using him or hurting his feelings.

The only thing to do, she decided, was be straight with him—have a nice dinner, be friendly, but make it clear it could be no more than that. No sexual encouragement, no seductions just to prove something—unlike some people she knew.... But she couldn't let herself think about Lance. It was too confusing and too upsetting.

One thing she *could* do was give herself a nice afternoon—or what was left of it. She soaked for an hour in a hot tub, then washed her hair carefully and brushed it dry, using the mini-blow dryer she traveled with. She realized she'd gotten into the same thing everyone did when touring—careless about dress and personal appearance. Not tonight, she thought. It was also the first time since the tour began that she'd really gone out to dinner with anyone, alone. The last time, she remembered, had been with Lance before the tour started.

She dabbed perfume on her wrists and neck, touched her eyes up with a little make-up, and applied lip gloss. The hot tub, perfume, and make-up all made her feel feminine. On a sudden whim she decided to wear the black dress she'd bought back in L.A. She stifled the knowledge that she'd bought it in the hope that one night she would wear it for Lance.

Putting it on, she had second thoughts. The back was cut low, and the skirt, cut on a bias, came up high on one leg. What if Derek got the wrong idea? Well if he did, she thought, she'd simply straighten him out. It had been too long since she'd worn a dress, too long since she'd looked and felt pretty. With a toss of her hair, she walked down to the hospitality room.

Low whistles greeted her as she walked in. Samson tossed down his comic book. "Hey, you look better than Wonder Woman."

January grinned appreciatively.

Joel and Teri were in the middle of a game of gin rummy. "Think Derek would like to trade dates tonight?" Joel said with a mischievous grin at his wife.

"I know I'd like to," said Teri, and then slapped her cards down. "Gin, lovey."

Joel moaned. "How come she always beats me?"

"She's smarter than you," said Samson. "Want a drink?" he asked January. "Bar's set up as usual."

January shook her head.

"Well, you better sit down and relax for a few minutes. When I left Derek he was going through agonies over what to wear."

Joek and Teri laughed.

"Be kind to him, January," said Teri. "He may propose tonight."

"Who's going to propose tonight?" said Lance, walking into the room. He saw January and looked her over appraisingly. "Where are you going?"

"Out with Derek," said Joel.

Lance looked at January. "Is that true?"

There was a silence in the room as the two faced each other.

"Of course it's true," said Teri.

"Did you get the amp fixed?" Samson asked.

Rick wandered in, looked at January but said nothing. "We fixed it."

"Maybe," Lance said. "It sounds okay now. I only hope it holds. We'll know tomorrow night."

"Maybe you should just replace it," January suggested.

"Maybe you should just mind your business," Lance said sharply. He turned on his heel and walked out of the room, brushing by Derek as he walked in.

"Wow," Derek said, seeing January. "You look great. What's eating Lance?"

"Thanks," January said. "Nothing. He's just edgy."

"You bet he is," Samson said, returning to his comic book.

"The amp okay?" Derek asked Rick.

"It's fine," he answered. "But next time, you guys, if anything is sounding wrong, come right to me. Don't go to Tim or one of the other guys."

Joel and Teri nodded as Derek apologized.

"No apologies necessary, man," Rick said. "The other roadies are . . . well . . . aw, forget it."

Samson hummed a phrase from Dylan's "Idiot Wind," and everyone laughed.

"Ready?" Derek asked January.

"Ready," she said.

"Don't stay up too late, children," Joel said.

"You look nice yourself," January said to Derek as they rode the elevator down to the lobby.

"Do you like Japanese food?" Derek asked as he helped her into a cab. "I heard about a place that's supposed to be pretty good, but we can go somewhere else if you prefer."

"Japanese is fine." Once again January experienced that hysterical urge to laugh. It had been a Japanese restaurant Lance had taken her to.

The restaurant was nice, the food delicious, the hot sake good, but Derek wasn't Lance. And January couldn't stop herself from wishing he was. Reminding herself that he was seriously involved with Kim did absolutely no good.

"Look," Derek said halfway through the meal, "I'm no dummy. I appreciate your going out with me, dressing so nicely and all, but I know you really have a thing for Lance, and it's okay."

January blushed. "I didn't think it was so obvious."

"It's not," said Derek. "But when you're interested in someone you become very aware of whether or not she likes you—or someone else. You like someone else. And you made him pretty angry tonight."

"He hasn't got any right to be angry," January said hotly.

"Nope, he hasn't, but he was jealous anyway. I know his eyes are green, but I've never seen them as green as they were tonight." Derek laughed. "It's probably good for him. He and Kim have been doing it to everyone else for years. About time he got some of his own back."

He and Kim have been doing it for years.

The words echoed back in January's mind later that night when she was back in her hotel room in bed.

After dinner, they'd gone out dancing and hadn't come

in until late. Teri was still up watching a horror movie. She walked January down to her room.

"Lance was here all night," she said. "He was furious. Seething. I guess he thought you two had begun to work something out this afternoon. Then when he saw you going out with Derek he almost flipped." Terri chuckled. "Good for him—a little of his own medicine."

"That's what Derek said."

"It's true. But mind you, don't give him too much. He is human after all." Teri smiled. "Got to get back to Dracula. See you in the morning."

As she was falling asleep, January wondered what difference it could possibly make to Lance if she went out with someone else.

The Providence shows went well, although there continued to be trouble with the amp. Rick said they should replace it, but Lance, in an uncharacteristic fit of stubbornness, said no, it was going to be okay. Rick shrugged and let it go.

January had friends in Providence, relatives of her mother. She spent most of her time with them. It was a relief to be away from the band, especially as Lance was tense and barely spoke to her. Often he seemed to refuse to acknowledge her presence and she was baffled, then infuriated. After all, she thought, what had she done? Gone out to dinner with Derek. Big deal.

On the bus from Providence to Boston, Teri said, "Lance better get his act together soon. He's pulling a spoiled star trip and it's a drag. If he doesn't want to talk to you," she said to January, "that's his business. But the amp thing is crazy. It's got to be replaced and he knows it."

"If he blows the Madison Square Garden gig," Joel said, "I personally will kill him."

January listened in silence, caught in an unexpected dilemma. Her next *Offbeat* article was due out soon. This kind of in-group trouble was exactly what Adrian would want her to put in. Backstage squabbling could always be sensed by astute critics when the group was onstage. If the band wasn't tight, everyone was going to know it. And if equipment wasn't working, the audience was going to be furious. The tour had gone well so far. A big turnout in Boston was almost guaranteed. And from there it was New York and Madison Square Garden, the benefit concert with the top rock groups in the country. They couldn't afford to mess up now. But if they did, January would have to write about it. As on-the-road-reporter, that was her job.

Her dilemma was the loyalty she had come to feel for Lance and for L. A. Expressway. She also knew that she was in some way involved in the present difficulties. Lance was angry at her, and even if she felt his anger was totally unfounded, it didn't alter anything. Lance's stubbornness about the amp was because of her. She knew it, and yet she didn't see what she could do about it.

Kim was waiting for them in Boston. She looked more beautiful than ever. While the rest of them had been on the road losing their L. A. tans, she had been back in California working on hers. Slim, bronzed, and glowing with health, she was lounging in the hospitality room of their Boston hotel, long legs slung up over the arm of a chair, lazily leafing through *Vogue* magazine.

"Where's Lance?" Samson asked.

Kim shrugged. "Out. Hello, January," she said coolly.

"Well, we need him here," Samson said. "We're playing tonight. We've got to check everything out."

"He'll be here," Kim said. "You guys have been getting great reviews."

"They're going to stink if we don't get that amp fixed," Joel muttered.

"Sound check at six," Rick said, wandering in. "You all better get some rest. Double show tonight, and they're both sold out. Livingston's coming into town to see the shows. Hi, Kim. Welcome back. Where's Lance?"

"No one knows," Derek said.

"I need him," Rick said, looking at January as if somehow Lance's disappearance was her fault.

"He'll show," said Teri. "I for one am getting out of here. I am going shopping; I am going to treat myself to a decent lunch; and then I'm going to a movie. Anyone want to come?"

"Sure," said Kim, unfolding herself from the armchair. "Love to."

"January?" Teri asked.

"No, thanks, I've got some stuff to do here." It wasn't true. She had been on the edge of accepting Teri's invitation but Kim got in too fast. There was nothing January would have liked more than to spend the day with Teri, indulging in girl talk. But there was no way she could handle an afternoon with Kim as well. Teri looked at her sympathetically, as if she knew what she was thinking.

"Okay," Teri said, "see you all later." She and Kim left.

"Anyone want to shoot some pool?" asked Joel. "There's a table downstairs."

"You're on," Samson said.

"Six o'clock," Rick yelled after them. "I got work to do," he said to Derek and January, the only ones left in the room. "Six o'clock," he repeated. "And if you see Lance, tell him to get over to the concert hall. I have to talk to him." He looked as if he wanted to say something more to January, but instead turned on his heel and left.

"That leaves you and me," Derek said. "What are you doing?"

"Going to my room, I guess," January said.

"There are some bookstores I want to check out. Want to come?"

"That'd be nice," January said with a grateful smile.

"Okay, I have some letters to write. How about meeting here in an hour?"

"Perfect."

"May I walk you to your room?" Derek asked with

a smile, and offered her his arm.

"Why thank you, sir." January gave a mock curtsy.

"You feel you're to blame about this stuff with Lance, don't you?" he asked as they walked down the hall.

"I do," said January. "I try not to. I know it's not really my fault, but I can't help feeling that way. And Rick doesn't make it any easier."

"Yeah, I know, but that's Rick. He feels it's his job to guard the band with his life, especially Lance. He's afraid you're going to hurt Lance—first, it was as a reporter; now it's as a woman."

"As a woman?" January laughed. "That's a good one."

Derek began to speak, but got out only a word or two because at that moment Lance himself came walking down the hall toward them.

January still had her arm linked through Derek's.

Lance stopped in front of them. "You two make a charming couple. Where is everybody?"

"Looking for you," Derek said. "Where've you been?"

Lance shrugged. "Out. Where's Kim?"

"Shopping with Teri," January said softly.

Lance didn't look at her. He addressed himself only to Derek.

"Joel and Samson are downstairs playing pool," said Derek, "and Rick's at the concert hall. He wants you over there."

"I'll go later," Lance said. "Jay Livingston's getting in in an hour. He's got the first releases of the album. I have to be here to meet him. We'll see how good a producer he really is. What time's sound check?"

"Six, but Rick needs you now."

"Rick can wait." And without another word Lance walked away.

January pulled her arm out of Derek's. "I've had enough of this," she said. "I don't think I'm going to make it to those bookstores with you. Sorry." She ran down the hall after Lance, caught his arm, and swung him around to face her before he knew what was happening. "Okay," she said. "Enough is enough. What is going on with you?"

"Let go of me," said Lance, pulling away from her.

"Oh no you don't," January said. "You're not getting away now."

"What do you want?"

"I want to know what's going on. Why you're being so damn stupid."

Lance looked at her, startled. "Stupid? What do you mean stupid?"

January had let go of his arms and was standing with her hands on her hips, eyes blazing. She forgot that they were in the middle of a corridor where anyone could hear them. "I mean stupid. Just because you're mad at me for no good reason doesn't mean you have to make the whole band suffer."

"Mad at you for no good reason?" Lance laughed cynically. "I'm not mad, January. Disillusioned maybe, but not mad. I really believed your 'I'm a traditional girl' story. You really had me fooled for a while there. Stupid. I was stupid all right. What are you going to do when you're finished with Derek, or things don't work out exactly the way you want them to? Move on to Samson? Or were you thinking of trying to get Joel away from Teri? How about Rick?"

January's face went white. "What are you talking about?"

Lance's green eyes were filled with disgust. "You know exactly what I'm talking about. Don't play Miss Innocent with me. You're worse than a groupie, January. At least groupies are honest about it. They don't pretend to be reporters."

This time as he turned away from her and marched down the hall January was incapable of moving. She felt frozen to the carpet. It seemed impossible that Lance could believe the things he'd said about her, and yet she knew he did. Slowly she turned and headed back to her room.

Derek was waiting down the hall for her, outside his

door. "I heard the things he said about you. They're not true. I know it. Everyone knows it. Even Lance knows it."

"Thanks," said January, wanting only to go to her room, close the door, and stay hidden behind it.

"You have to understand," said Derek. "Lance is in—"

"Please," January said, "not now. Really. I just want to be alone."

"Okay," Derek said. "If you need anything, you know where I am."

January nodded, went to her room, and shut the door. Four more days, she said to herself, four more days and it's all over. Three days in Boston, one in New York, and then home!

And at that moment, to go home was the only thing on earth she wanted.

As soon as she walked into the auditorium for that night's show, January sensed something wrong. The mood of the audience was different. There was a jaded quality, a sense of We've-heard-so-much-about-you-now-show-us-what-you-can-do. All the other audiences had been open and receptive. This one wanted to see L. A. Expressway fail.

It wasn't an uncommon phenomenon. It happened sooner or later to every band and no one knew where it would be or why. It could be Topeka, Kansas, or Gallup, New Mexico; because of a full moon or no moon at all. Such audiences were inevitable and unpredictable. Sometimes the band could win them over, sometimes not. It depended on the amount of energy the group was willing to expend, and on the malleability of the people who had come to see the show. It was never easy to "get" an audience that didn't want to be "gotten" but it could be done.

January found herself sitting with her fingers crossed as she waited for Lance to come out. All animosity was forgotten. She wanted him to play well. She wanted him to get those Bostonians in the palm of his hand and have them screaming for more. She knew he could do it.

Applause was scanty as the house lights dimmed and the stage lights went on. There were a few catcalls. Someone screamed an obscenity. January knew the atmosphere backstage without being there: the tension, the nerves, the edginess that came with having to face a mass of anonymous people who were against you.

Between the time the house lights went down and the band came on, there was a delay, during which the audience grew more restless. When they did walk out, someone up front called, "Where ya been?"

"Taking a nap," Lance said with a grin into the microphone. There was some laughter, a little applause, and then someone else yelled, "Well, wake up!" The remark drew more laughs and applause than Lance's. It was an audience that loved itself.

Lance paid no attention. He went right into the opening song, slamming his hand down on his guitar. And it was at that point, January thought afterward, that the nightmare really began.

Guitar strings inevitably break. But a string breaking on the first chord of the first song is enough to drive anyone crazy. Lance didn't even bother to change it. He played the first song through with a missing string. At the end of it Rick ran out with a second guitar. The audience was jeering and whistling. But Lance ignored them.

Sometimes a gimmick like that could work. Losing the butt of their jokes, the audience would grow quiet and start paying attention. Not this time. A few people got up and left. The bad amp gave out. The audience was hissing. Lance wasn't even playing; the band was trying to fill in but half the sound they were making was lost. When the jeers and catcalls grew louder, Lance simply walked off the stage.

January held her breath. She couldn't believe it. Lance couldn't be so unprofessional that he'd just quit like that, leaving the band—each member a close, old friend—to fend for itself before this hostile audience. Her heart was beating furiously, her stomach churning so much she thought she might be sick. She closed her eyes briefly. Lack of professionalism wasn't the half of it . . . it was lack of courage. She'd thought Lance was a man she could admire . . . despite her suspicions about him borne of his profession, despite his confusing relationship with Kim. She simply couldn't stand the idea he was a coward! The very idea was a hot knife slicing through her middle. She jumped to her feet, intent on bolting out of the auditorium and getting out to the cool, fresh night. But she sat again just as quickly as she'd risen. The house lights had come up full for a second and then been extinguished. The footlights hadn't been on for the performance, but now they were, low and giving just enough light to show the dramatic drop of the curtain obscuring the band and cutting off their last notes as its fringed edges swept the stage floor.

Over! January thought with a sinking heart. They were just bringing down the curtain and calling it quits. A worse ending to this disastrous concert than she could have imagined. In a second the exodus would start. People in the audience, irate and feeling they'd been ripped off, would begin to jostle and shove their way out of the auditorium to demand their money back from the box-office workers. What would Jay Livingston do?

But no one left his seat. There was a smoky blue spotlight dancing over the curtain. The air of tension and suspense grew. What was going to happen? A drop of a pin could be heard—no one even coughed in the filled auditorium. And then the spot darted to the wings—to Lance! He had a mike clipped to the open vee of a cream silk shirt; the fingers of his right hand grasped the throat of his guitar. He ambled to center stage, but though his movements were slow, casual—almost leisurely—there was leashed power in his walk, an air of command authority that was undeniable.

January's eyes filled with tears of pride and she was so choked up she could scarcely swallow.

Lance planted his feet wide apart and looked over the audience. January knew he couldn't see more than the faces in the first few rows and then it was a sea of blackness he gazed into. But it didn't seem that way. It seemed his eyes made contact with every other pair of eyes in that entire vast audience. He held them at once shaming them and shackling them. At last he spoke.

"That great old American philosopher Thoreau said something that's filling my mind tonight. 'Could a greater miracle take place than for us to look through each other's eyes for an instant?' Let's make a pact. Let's try. Music's the miracle anyway, you know. At least it is for me."

He started with soft ballads, lyrical and expressive. Just the guitar and the voice. Lance put himself on the line and didn't pull any tricks—no gyrating, no hyped emotionality. He sang lyric after lyric with precision and sincerity and the audience stayed with him, then began to turn toward him. He stopped, looked to the back of the audience, and said, "This is for my lady—just the way I wrote it." Of course he launched into "Diamonds of the Sea" then and brought the crowd to scattered applause. January was moved, so moved she was trembling. The song sounded so different, but so heartfelt without the backup of the group.

At the end the audience belonged to Lance, belonged to him heart and soul . . . and they were cheering wildly. He raised a hand calling for quiet.

"Now a new one I'm trying out. Each one of you will be the second person to hear it. No lyrics yet, so just stick with me."

And then he was playing the melody he'd hummed for January that last afternoon after they'd made rapturous love. Tears streamed down her face and when he'd finished and was walking offstage she found herself on her feet yelling as loudly as the people around her.

Lance didn't come out for an encore. He had turned a near-tragedy into triumph and he left his audience begging for more of him. January couldn't wait to get backstage. She was bursting with happiness for Lance and pride in the character he'd displayed. The stage door was jammed; it seemed to take forever to push her way through and then only to discover that Lance had vanished. Everyone was in a stew, especially the producer, Jay Livingston.

"Damn," he kept muttering. "The biggest night for publicity I can remember and Lance has taken a powder on us."

Kim and Rick volunteered to search for Lance and left. The rest of the band sat watching Jay pace around, rubbing his hands and looking like a gleeful kid.

"We're going to make some public statements on the radio tomorrow. We're going to get Lance instant interviews and put him in whatever Boston's biggest record shop is, hyping the album, giving copies away. We're going to make this whole evening the biggest thing that's happened in music since the Beatles' first tour. We're going to turn it into a huge publicity stunt."

"Excuse me if I look skeptical," said Joel, "but I do believe if anyone can pull it off, you can."

"I can and I will," Jay said. "January, I'm going to need your help. "We've got to start calling radio stations to set up interviews with Lance for tomorrow." He pulled out a list. "We have to go through these, see how many will take our statements or give us airplay." He glanced at her. "I'm not asking you to do anything unethical— only make the calls and see if they'll either put Lance on their shows, take a statement from him, or play his music."

"Or all three," Samson said.

"Or all three," Jay agreed. He grinned. "Well, I guess it is if not unethical, at least a little unorthodox. I'm asking you to be our private press agent at the moment."

"Where's Diane?" January asked.

"Never here when you need her," Teri said. "She hasn't been around since Washington. Haven't you noticed?"

"Will you do it?" Jay asked.

"I will," January replied, "but I'll have to report it in my *Offbeat* article. It's only fair."

"No problem," Jay said. "Any other volunteers?"

The rest of the band chipped in to help. It was almost two in the morning when they'd finished calling radio stations. Some of the all-night stations were willing to make immediate announcements; others were willing to interview Lance the next day.

"Now he better show up," Derek said.

At that moment Kim and Rick walked in looking exhausted.

"No sign of him," they said together.

"Well," said Jay, "we've done all we can tonight. We better all get some sleep. He'll show up sooner or later."

"It's going to have to be sooner," Samson said. "His first interview is at nine tomorrow morning."

They filed to their rooms slowly, all of them more worried about why Lance had gone off alone and where he was than they cared to let on.

January turned the key in her door, let herself into her room, reached for the light switch.

"Don't turn it on," a voice said in the darkness.

January almost jumped out of her skin. "Who is it?" she said. "Who's there?"

"Who do you think?"

"Lance?"

"Who else?" he said.

She realized he must be lying on her bed. "How did you get in here?" she asked.

"I had the hotel manager let me in ages ago. I told him you were my girlfriend and that I'd left something in your room. He knew we were all traveling together."

Gradually January's eyes adjusted to the light. A red

and blue neon sign across the way cast a strange lavender glow in the room by which she was able to make out Lance's form on her bed.

"Where've you been?" he asked.

"That's what everyone's been asking about you," she said, recovering from the shock of finding him in her room. "Where've you been?"

"Right here," Lance said.

She was still standing by the door. He held out a hand to her. "Come and sit by me," he said.

She didn't move. "Do you realize you've driven everyone just about half crazy tonight?" she asked angrily. "Kim and Rick have been all over the place looking for you. The rest of us have spent the night calling every radio station in the city and lining up interviews. Reporters want to talk to you, don't you realize? For your information, you have five interviews to do tomorrow, starting at nine in the morning."

Lance laughed softly. "I love it when you get angry."

"Oh shut up," said January. "What are you doing here, anyway? This is my room in case you hadn't noticed."

"I know exactly whose room this is. January, come here."

She walked over to the bed. "What?" she said.

"I wanted somewhere I felt safe," Lance said. "Somewhere I felt I could be left alone, undisturbed. It was a close thing tonight, January... it took a helluva lot out of me... and really made me think. About a lot more than the music business, too. I came straight here from the auditorium and I gave the manager strict orders not to tell anyone. I figured the only place no one would look for me would be in your room."

"You were right about that," said January. "We searched everywhere else."

"May I sleep here?" he asked.

"I should tell Jay at least where you are, or that I've seen you."

"Go ahead," Lance said, "but no one else. And no

explanations, not right now."

January called Jay to let him know she'd seen Lance, that he'd be there for the interviews, and that that was all she could say at the moment. Then she turned to Lance. "You owe me an explanation, at least."

"I told you. I thought this was the safest place. And I trust you."

"Really?" January said. "Yesterday you told me I was just a groupie. Or was that today? You change your tunes so often I can't keep track of them anymore."

"I apologize for that." He reached a hand to her but she wouldn't take it. "You and Derek would never be anything but friends. I know that. I was jealous."

"Jealous?" said January. "What right have you to be jealous? You're the one with Kim."

"I never finished explaining that..."

"Lance, it's almost three in the morning. I've heard enough tonight. I've been through enough. And—more important—so have you. You need rest, so why don't you give me the key to your room?"

"Sleep here."

"You're in my bed."

"Sleep with me. Just sleep. Nothing more."

Evidently Lance had forgotten she'd come to him only a few days ago practically begging him to touch her. It wasn't him she didn't trust—it was herself.

"We'll sleep side by side on the top of the bed fully dressed," he said, "like little kids."

"Lance..."

He swung himself off the bed to stand beside her. Sometime during the evening he'd gone to his room long enough to change out of his performance clothes into a pair of jeans. He wasn't wearing a shirt. He put an arm around January. "Come on," he said. "You're tired, I'm tired. We'll sleep."

Involuntarily she let him lead her to the bed.

"Lie on your stomach," he ordered. "I know I said I wouldn't touch you, but this'll help you relax. After all the time you put into my career tonight, I owe you."

He began kneading the muscles of her shoulders, neck, and back. His hands felt wonderful on her, soothing away the tension. Everything felt warm, velvety dark. She drifted into sleep. And awoke early the next morning, to see Lance still in his jeans, leaning on an elbow looking at her. He had pulled a cover over her.

"I took your shoes and slacks off last night. I thought you'd be more comfortable."

She looked at him drowsily. "I don't even remember falling asleep."

He grinned. "You were gone in about two seconds."

"What time is it?"

"Seven-thirty. I've already talked to Jay this morning. I hear you've become my press secretary."

"Not really. Only to help out last night. I do work for *Offbeat,* you know."

"I know. I can't wait to see what story you write about this."

"About what?"

There was a mischievous glint in his eye. "Our sleeping together."

January groaned and sat up. "What am I going to say? To everyone else? To Kim?"

"Forget about Kim," said Lance. "We're not saying anything to anyone. I was out all night. That's all anyone needs to know. How about some breakfast? Coffee, juice, eggs?" He dialed room service. "You have work to do today. Since you're my new official press secretary, you have to come to all my interviews with me."

"Lance . . ."

"What?"

"Oh, never mind," January said, not even sure what she wanted to say. Seeing him sitting on the edge of her bed, shirtless, sun coming in on his bare shoulders, hair tousled as he ordered their breakfast, she realized she was so totally in love with him that nothing mattered. And she was content.

That feeling of contentment went on all day as they went with Jay from radio station to radio station and finally, at two o'clock that afternoon, to one of Boston's largest record stores. Jay had had a special shipment of the new album flown in overnight. Kids were lined up to buy the record and see the heroic Lance Devlin. Lance spent three hours giving autographs until at last he said he had to quit or he'd never be able to play the guitar that night. January was at his side the whole time, and although it occasionally crossed her mind it should be Kim, she didn't fret about it. All day Lance was relaxed, easy and joking with her, and she with him.

The shows that night were a great success and so were the next night's. The story of L.A. Expressway's total failure followed by total success was in all the Boston papers. The crisis served to bring the whole band closer together than they had been before, almost as if it had had a purging effect. After their last show in Boston, they felt ready for New York—nervous, apprehensive, but eager and excited. Some of the country's biggest stars were going to be playing: Carly Simon, James Taylor, Bruce Springsteen.

"Madison Square Garden," Samson said. "It's really going to happen."

Only January wasn't dancing with joy. Lance was with Kim a great deal again. January knew she had no right to feel let down or disappointed, but she did. She had liked falling asleep with him rubbing her back, liked waking up with him the next morning, having breakfast together. The pleasure of being with him went far beyond sex. She wanted to be his friend, his lover, his...she refused to let herself think about permanence. There was always Kim, Kim who had a special call on Lance.

One morning she knocked on his door early with a message for him from Jay.

"Come on in," said Kim, opening the door. "Oh it's you," she said, seeing January. "What can I do for you?"

"I have a message for Lance from Jay."

Kim looked January over coolly then called out in a clear voice, "Lance—it's January. He's in the bathroom," she explained.

As January waited she couldn't help noticing that the room had two double beds—and that both of them had been slept in. What was it between Kim and Lance? She was determined to find an opportunity soon to have that long-postponed discussion with Lance on the subject.

The bathroom door swung open. Lance came out, a towel wrapped around his waist, his hair damp. "Did you call me?"

Abruptly January remembered the shower they'd taken together.

Kim indicated January. "She has a message for you from Jay."

January gave Lance the message.

"No problem," said Lance. "Tell him I'll be down in ten minutes. I've got to shave." He gave January a peck on the cheek and went back into the bathroom.

Kim held the door for her. "See you around." January nodded and started down the hall. "Hey," said Kim, running after her. January stopped. "Could we talk sometime? Have lunch? I'd like to get some things straight with you. About the beds..."

"I'm pretty busy," said January.

"Lunch," said Kim.

"I don't think so."

"Okay," said Kim, "have it your way." She shrugged. "Just trying to do you a favor."

"No, thanks."

As she hurried down the hallway, she could feel Kim watching her. The last thing she wanted to do was have lunch with her, listen to her talk about Lance.

January tried to reason with herself: the night he spent with her in her room, he had made no attempt to make love with her. He needed solitude, peace, and her room had been it—that was all.

But the rationalizations didn't make her feel any better. On the bus to New York all the band, Lance and Kim included, were feeling up and excited, telling jokes and making wisecracks. She was silent, sitting slightly apart.

Teri noticed and asked if anything was wrong.

January shook her head. "Tired," she said, "that's all." Lance threw her a concerned look and came over to sit beside her.

"You okay?" he asked.

"Fine, really. Traveling fatigue, I guess."

"Traveling blues," said Lance. He covered her hand with his. "We all get them."

January saw Kim watching them, but Lance didn't let go of her hand. "I'm all right," she said, wishing he'd go away. Even his hand in hers set up a quivering in her body she was scared he'd detect.

But he stayed at her side, talking softly so the others couldn't hear. Samson was organizing a game of poker. Kim joined in.

"I haven't had a chance to talk to you at all," said Lance. "Not even to thank you properly for all you did."

January started to protest but he cut her off.

"It's been really hectic. Everyone's gearing up for the New York show. Energy sizzling. We're like live wires right now. But after the show it'll be different. I want to spend time with you—just the two of us." His hand tightened on hers; his voice dropped lower. "Can you stay on in New York for a few days?"

January's heart raced.

"Get some time off?"

Adrian had told her to take a few days off if she wanted.

"I'd like to be with you."

They would be together, stay in New York, fly back to Los Angeles...

"First," Lance was saying, "I have to spend a few days with Kim, but then after that..."

"No," January said abruptly, extricating her hand from his, speaking quietly but firmly. "I can't. I'd love to, but I have to be back in L.A. the next day. I've got another assignment. I'm sorry. It would be really nice but..."

There was a slightly hurt look in Lance's eyes as he said, "No, that's okay. I understand."

"Adrian wants me back."

"I understand," Lance said. "Well, maybe when I get back into L. A. I can see you there."

"Sure," January said, "why not?" Knowing he'd never call, knowing she'd never hear from him again.

"Okay," Lance said. He looked at her strangely for a minute as if trying to fathom what was really going on inside her, and then moved away. He sat down beside Kim to join the poker game.

January had a terrible urge to cry which took all her strength to choke back.

Dreamer, she told herself, as she looked out the bus windows. Stupid, foolish dreamer. You really thought for a moment he wanted you, that you were going to be together. What did you think he was going to do with Kim? Drop her by the wayside?

She made up her mind as the bus raced down the highway, through tunnels in granite cliffs, past green fields, that she wasn't spending an extra minute in New York. She would fly out the very next night, right after the concert, on the first flight she could get. The only thing she wanted was to be back at home, in her own house, in her own office, away from Lance, away from everything, in her nice safe world. She turned her gaze away from the highway to the card table that the band was gathered around. Lance had his arm around Kim. They were laughing together.

chapter

12

"TWENTY MINUTES," Rick was calling out to the band. "Twenty minutes and we're on."

"Nervous?" January asked Lance.

"A wreck. Where's Kim?"

"Up front with Jay."

"They save you a seat?"

January nodded. She was backstage with Lance at his request before they went on. It had taken her by surprise when he'd asked her earlier that day in the hotel to be there—for good luck, he had said. Then he'd grinned his quirky, devilish grin, and added that she could pick up some local color for her final story.

Local color there was and in plenty. Madison Square Garden was packed to capacity, and backstage was milling with musicians, some of them rock's most recognizable faces; others, like Lance, less known. At a benefit concert like this, groups only played for two or three numbers. Lance was scheduled to follow Carly Simon, who was on now.

"You'll do fine," January said. "The audience is there for you. They're going crazy as it is. Just give them your best shot."

"Be here after the concert—there's a party. I have to take Kim along and I want you, too."

January couldn't help smiling to herself. As usual Lance wanted everything—her, Kim, the works. She nodded. She didn't bother to tell him she was taking a flight out that night. After the show, he'd be flying so high that he'd never notice if she were there or not. Right now, she was willing to say yes to anything as long as it would keep him calmed down. She loved him; she wanted him to be a smash . . . no matter the cost to her personally.

They were standing in the wings watching Carly Simon perform.

"She's great, isn't she?" said Lance.

Beyond the stage was a sea of faces, tier upon tier of wildly enthusiastic spectators, barely discernible through the lights that poured down onto the stage. But the energy could be felt, the energy of thousands of people giving themselves to the pulsating rhythms.

"I've never played a place this big," Lance whispered.

Instinctively January took his hand and felt his fingers grip hers in return.

Simon was finishing her last song. Already the road crew was getting ready to set up L.A. Expressway's equipment even as Simon's people prepared to remove hers.

Lance turned January to face him.

The audience was on its feet applauding as Carly, with a toss of her long hair, left the stage. Immediately a casually dressed man got up onstage to talk about why they were all there, what their money was going to, how important the cause was. He kept them listening as the stage was readied for the next group.

Lance put his arms around January. "Thank you for being back here with me tonight," he whispered in her hair. He drew her closer. "There's so much I want to say to you. Later, after the show . . . Kim's . . ."

The noise from the audience was deafening as they cheered something the speaker said. January could barely make out what Lance was saying to her. The words were lost in the confusion.

"A pact we made . . . three days . . ."

January strained to hear.

Rick tapped Lance's shoulder. "Three minutes."

"Promise?" Lance said to January.

Promise what, she wondered, unable to hear him at all now. She nodded anyway.

His arms tightened around her. "Say yes," he said to her, "promise me yes."

The band was ready to go out.

"Yes," said January quickly, having no idea what she was saying yes to, not caring, knowing only she had to appease Lance and get him out onstage.

He bent his head. His lips found hers. His mouth was soft, tender. He was kissing her as if he had all the time in the world, only this to do and nothing else, and she was melting, almost faint, almost having forgotten what it was like to be kissed by Lance, having not allowed herself to be conscious of how much she yearned for his kisses. He kept on kissing her as if he wanted to weld her to him.

"Break it up," Rick said, pulling Lance away. "You're on."

Abruptly January found herself standing alone in the wings, only stagehands around her. What had seemed like the roar of the ocean in her ears became once more the sound of the crowd. The hazy blue light was stage lighting. Lance and L. A. Expressway were out onstage breaking into their first song. January stood a few moments longer watching from the wings. Lance's lithe body seemed to glide across the stage as he moved to the music of his opening piece. Teri's voice was soaring up over his, creating incredible harmonies. The band sounded great. January knew it; the whole audience knew it. Even from the wings she could sense the mood up front, the enthusiasm Lance was generating. For a second, Lance seemed to glance over in her direction. For a second he seemed to see her and smile. But she couldn't be sure, and then he was turned away, playing to the audience, making his guitar sing to them, making his body move for them.

January hurried out the side exit and around to the seat Kim and Jay had saved for her. Kim was bouncing up and down in her seat, hair waving, loudly cheering. If she minded that it had been January backstage with Lance, she certainly didn't show it.

"He's got 'em," Jay was whispering, "he's got 'em. Madison Square Garden and he's got them in the palm of his hand." The producer was grinning like a lunatic.

January, too, was swept up in the energy and excitement, clapping and whistling between songs with the crowd. Once again, as in Boston, she allowed the reporter side of her to go dead and let herself become one with the audience. At the end of the third and last song of the set she heard her own voice screaming for an encore as loud as anyone's. Grinning, Lance obliged.

"This song," he yelled out, "is for January." There was a roar of approval from the audience. Everyone knew what was coming. As he went into "Diamonds of the Sea," all of Madison Square Garden rose to its feet and cheered.

January looked on in amazement. Adrian had been right—Lance and the group had just become what the press would later call an overnight success. He was a star. And as she too rose to her feet, she realized that even though she'd been on the tour the whole way, she couldn't say what had happened. The momentum had built; for a minute it had looked like everything had crashed, but they'd pulled through, pulled themselves up, and now they were a phenomenon. Lance had made it, in that strange way that stars did—one minute almost invisible, the next glowing brightly over everyone's heads. And January knew that in the minds of most of the people here they were the alchemists who had made this particular star shine tonight. The rest of the concert would go on; bigger, more famous groups would play before the evening ended; but this audience had chosen Lance as theirs. They had launched him, set him out there to glitter above all the others. Tomorrow they might forget him, but tonight was his.

Twenty-four hours later, January was at her desk typing up the story.

As she wrote it, she tried to piece the facts together, to pinpoint the moment that had guaranteed Lance his night, but she couldn't. Nor could she figure out how it was that when "Diamonds" had finally been openly dedicated to her the audience had cheered. The more she tried to write, the more confused she became.

"You're not on the outside of the story anymore," Adrian said. "You're a part of it. Write it that way." He studied her face. "Better yet, don't write it at all, at least not for a few days. You're exhausted. Why didn't you stay in New York like I told you to, or go somewhere for a rest?"

"I wanted to get home."

"A man dedicates a song to you at Madison Square Garden and you want to get home?" Adrian stared at her incredulously.

January reached into her desk drawer and pulled out a copy of one of the daily gossip tabloids. She slapped it down in front of him. "This is how much that dedication meant," she said.

The cover photo, full page, was of Lance and Kim arm in arm. Underneath the photo, the caption read: "Lance Devlin, Music's New Sensation, and Actress Kim Chiles Do the Town."

"This is the story everywhere," said January. "Kim and Lance. Okay? So lay off me, Adrian. Lance was grateful for the good coverage the band got from me and the extra help I gave them in Boston. That's all."

"I suppose," said Adrian thoughtfully, "that I have to take your word for it, don't I?"

"You do," said January.

"All right, fine, but now take my word for this. Until you get some sleep, some food, some proper rest, you're never going to be able to write a decent story. So go home, would you? I don't need you around here."

January took a deep breath and acquiesced. She didn't want to tell Adrian that home was the last place she wanted to be.

Once alone she found that all she thought of was the lonely flight across the country. She had headed from the Garden straight out to the airport, having already sent her bag ahead, and had gotten on the first flight available. As the lights of New York had been left behind, she had had a sinking feeling of leaving something infinitely precious.

She kept remembering Lance's kiss, his touch, his smile, his laugh, his voice, the way he walked, the way he talked. And she remembered being in bed with him: the feel of his skin against hers, the strength of his muscles as he held her; the hardness of his body and the tenderness of his caresses. She felt a wave of longing go through her. As much as she tried to steel herself against that aching desire, it still swept through her. And as much as she tried to resign herself to the fact that it was over with Lance, that it hadn't really *been* at all, she couldn't. All night she sat in the plane remembering every moment, every second with him, each tiny detail and minute gesture.

She took a cab home from the airport and, glad as she was to see her house and her garden all in good order, thanks to Alicia, the ache continued inside her. Still unable to sleep and jittery from all the traveling, she went straight into the office, where Adrian looked at her askance and asked what on earth she was doing there. She simply replied that she had a story to write and wanted to get it done. But by the end of the day, she hadn't been able to write it and that was when Adrian told her to go home.

The phone was ringing when she walked into the house. She took a deep breath before answering it, telling herself it wasn't Lance, it couldn't be Lance, and hoping against hope that it was.

"Hello," she said, keeping her voice even.

"January, this is Kim." Kim's voice was hard, cold. Before January could say anything, Kim went on. "I think what you did to Lance was downright cruel. Not only that, it was deceitful. You promised him."

"Kim, I . . ."

"Look," interrupted Kim. "Lance doesn't know I'm calling. He'd never call you himself. You've made it pretty clear how you feel, but I wanted to tell you because I care about him. I love him and I don't like to see the people I love being messed around with. And January, one more thing—when Lance gets back into town, stay away from him. He doesn't need people like you in his life." There was silence, a click, and then the dial tone. Kim had hung up.

January stood, the receiver in her hand, not knowing what to think. What had she done, she wondered. Slowly she set the receiver back in place, thinking of calling Kim back at the hotel in New York, somehow knowing it was pointless. She vaguely remembered Lance asking her to promise him something and her saying yes only to silence him, to appease him, and get him out onstage. But it couldn't have been important, not with him doing the town with Kim.

She suddenly realized her hands were shaking, her whole body was trembling. She took a couple of deep breaths to relax herself and sank down into an armchair. Take it easy, she told herself, feeling she was about to cry, take it easy.

The phone rang again. It was Alicia.

"January, how are you? What are you doing back so soon? I thought you were going to stay on in New York.

Don't you and Lance have a thing going? He's been dedicating all his songs to you."

"Alicia, please . . ."

"January, are you all right?"

"I'm fine. A little tired, maybe, but . . ."

"You sound exhausted. Adrian said you were but I didn't believe him. You know how he exaggerates. Do you need anything? Some soup? Let me come over and fix you something to eat."

"Okay," said January weakly, giving in. She hadn't the strength to fight Alicia nor, she suspected, did she even have the strength to feed herself. All of a sudden the only thing she wanted to do was collapse in bed—which she did.

For three days she stayed there letting Alicia take care of her.

"Damn tours," said Alicia. "You shouldn't do them. They're too draining."

"I'm okay," said January on the third day of hearing Alicia repeat the same thing over and over. "I'm going to work tomorrow. I have to, I haven't done that story."

Alicia looked at her, running a hand through her tousled blond hair. "Are you sure you're ready?"

January smiled. "As ready as I'll ever be. Three days of rest and being looked after was just what I needed."

Alicia sat down on the side of the bed. "Did you fall in love with Lance?" she asked abruptly.

"You get right to the point, don't you?" said January. "Yes, I suppose I did."

"No 'suppose' about it. You did or you didn't."

"Okay, yes, I did."

"Then what are you doing here? Why aren't you in New York with him? Or somewhere, anywhere. Why'd you come back?"

"He's not in love with me, Alicia."

"He dedicates all his songs to you. The whole country knows."

"Yes," January said bitterly, "and the whole country now knows that he's with Kim Chiles, and has been all along. I don't know why he dedicates those songs to me, Alicia, but believe me, it's Kim he loves, not me."

"Did you go to bed with him?" Alicia asked compassionately.

January sighed, a long, heavy sigh. "Yes." And as she said it, all the pain that she'd been holding back flooded her and she burst into tears.

Alicia instantly put her arms around her and held her. "It's okay," she crooned. "I know how you feel. It's okay. Go ahead and cry."

"Every man I love," January sniffed, "after a while, I lose—my father, Mike, and now Lance. How come it never works out for me, Alicia?" she said, drying her tears.

"It'll work out for you," said Alicia, "I guarantee it will. Are you sure about him and Kim?"

January nodded.

Alicia shook her head. "I find it hard to believe. Adrian and I have known Lance awhile—he was never the two-timing kind. And I didn't think he and Kim were serious. They've been good friends for years, but never more than that. Oh, they pretended it was more because they thought it was fun and it kept other people from bothering them, but . . ."

"Wait a minute," said January, sitting up. "What do you mean you've known Lance for a while?"

"Adrian's known him longer . . ."

"Adrian never told me he knew Lance."

"He wanted you to come to the story fresh. He didn't want your writing to be biased just because he was. He's been following Lance's career for years. Up until this tour, Lance asked him not to do anything on them."

"Why was Lance so hostile that first day in my office then?" asked January.

"The agreement was, I believe, that Lance would treat you exactly as he'd treat any reporter. He did hate the press; all that hostility was real. The only person he trusted was Adrian. After that first story came out, he was ready to shoot Adrian as well. Lance is a very loyal person, and he expects the same loyalty from others. He felt Adrian had not only betrayed him professionally but personally as well. It was you, whatever you did, that got that whole mess straightened out for everyone."

January remembered the day she had been yelling at Adrian on the phone and Lance had been outside her door. That was the same day she and Lance had almost made love. Her body went hot at the memory.

Alicia glanced at her watch. "I have to go. Listen, it's impossible for me to accept that Kim and Lance are lovers, no matter what you say. There's some kind of a complicated story there—but not a love story! The rest of the band is going to be back in town today or tomorrow. Let me do a little sleuthing on my own, okay?"

January shrugged. "Sure, if you want to, but, Alicia, don't get your hopes up."

"Ha," said Alicia, "it's not my hopes I'm concerned about, it's yours. They're the ones I want to raise."

January grinned. "They'll rise of their own accord. I feel much better already. You're a great friend."

"Be a good one to me," said Alicia. "Take one more day off. Get some sun. You look like a ghost. And eat something. You're too thin."

January gave her a quick salute. "You got it, boss."

Adrian called her the next morning to repeat Alicia's orders to take one more day off and January complied.

She spent the day lying in the hot sun, working in her garden, and washing her clothes. She was putting freshly laundered shirts away in her bureau drawer when she heard the doorbell ring.

"Teri," she said with surprise as she opened the door.

"We got in last night," Teri said, walking straight into the living room and plunking herself down on the sofa. "Alicia called today. She said you'd been sick."

"Not sick, just tired."

"You look okay to me," said Teri, studying her. "A little thin maybe. I've got jet lag and after-tour shakes, but otherwise I'm doing fine. Alicia told me where you lived. I hope you don't mind my barging in on you like this."

January shook her head.

"Why'd you do that to Lance?" said Teri.

"Do what?"

"Walk out on him like that, after you'd promised you'd stay."

January sat down on the sofa beside Teri. "So that's what I promised. How long did I say I'd stay for?"

Teri was staring at her. "You mean you don't know?"

"No. There was so much noise backstage. Lance was telling me to promise him something. He was supposed to go on. I said yes. I figured it didn't matter what it was. All I knew was I had to get him out on that stage. I'd have said yes to anything at that moment."

"Well, you promised him you'd stay in New York and then go somewhere with him for a week or so."

"Really?" said January caustically. "And what was he intending to do with Kim?"

"What about Kim?" Teri said. "She'd come back here. This is where she lives, where her boyfriend is."

"What?" January said.

"Oh, January, you *never* got it all out of Lance!" She moaned and held her head. "Of course he'd be reluctant to blurt it all out. I mean, it's Kim's story, a lot of which isn't pretty. And Lance wouldn't want to toot his own horn. There's so much for you to *know*, hon!"

"Know?"

"Kim and Lance are like Lance and me, but with a difference—a really important difference. We all grew up together, next door to one another or down the block. We were all best friends. We took baths together, stayed at each other's houses for the night. The whole works. Lance and I made music together. Kim and Lance made trouble together." Teri paused as if trying to skip through time to see when—exactly—she should pick up the story again. "All that smooching and pretending to get it on together—it's a game. I think they tried it once, seriously, in high school, to be boyfriend and girlfriend, but it didn't work. For a long time they've done that act in front of other people to keep the lechers away from her and the groupies away from him."

"They sleep together," January said.

"Sure," said Teri, "in the same room, not the same bed. I thought Lance explained all this to you."

January was remembering the two beds and all the times Lance, Derek, Teri, everyone, even Kim, had tried to talk to her and she'd refused to listen. "He tried," she said quietly.

"You two are something else," said Teri. "Nothing like lack of communication. You're a writer, he's a musician. That's what you two are meant to be best at, communicating, and you can't even talk to each other."

"Right," January snorted. "I'm just great at communicating." She frowned. "There's a lot more, Teri, but my instincts tell me you're nervous about telling it."

Teri shook her head vehemently. "Let me say it real fast. About a year and a half ago Kim went through several bad scenes, one right after the other. And, as my dear old mom would say, she fell in with the wrong company."

"Aw, Lord," January burst out. "Drugs!"

"Yeah. You got it. Lance was like a crazy man when he found out. He pulled her out of a lousy place, took her home, and helped her get straight. Whenever she's afraid, whenever she's got this 'falling feeling,' she runs to Lance."

January was shaking her head. "I feel like a heel. And a stupid, insensitive, rotten—"

"Stop it," Teri said firmly. "What do you get from dumping on yourself like that? Look, it's almost over with Kim and Lance. He had her pretty much on the road to being weaned from him. But this thing with you may have been a blessing in disguise."

"A blessing?"

"Sure," Teri said. "See, for the first time Lance was in trouble. He was broken and he needed Kim. I think she'll have grown a *lot* stronger from this."

"Why didn't I figure out some of this?" January asked dejectedly.

Teri laughed. "I suppose you never figured out either that Lance is madly, deeply in love with you."

January shook her head.

"Well, he is," said Teri, "or was. Right now he feels betrayed by you. His usual thing. Of course, no one knows where he is. Once he spent those three days with Kim, he took off—no one's heard from him since."

"Okay," said January. "Before we have yet another misunderstanding, what were those three days with Kim about?"

"Lance had always promised Kim that if he became famous first they would spend three days together doing the town and making sure they got in every paper."

"They succeeded at that," January said.

Teri grinned. "Of course. And if Kim had become famous first, she'd have done it for Lance. That was their deal. You know, you ought to try to get to know Kim. Underneath she is a very warmhearted, giving person. And she's the sister Lance always wanted and never had. All of us in the band are like brothers and sisters. He's crazed for big families, always was, always will be."

"I feel like a fool," January said. "What do I do now?"

"Good question," Teri said. "I guess when Lance gets back into town we'll try to convince him to come see you—providing, of course, you want to see him."

"I do," said January softly, "more than anything in the world. But where's he gone?"

"No one knows. He did his old trick of taking off and disappearing. He left a note for us and that was all: 'Gone on vacation, Love, Lance,' with no clue as to where he'd gone. He didn't even tell Kim."

"So what do I do?" January said.

"The same thing the rest of us do," Teri replied. "Sit around and wait to hear from him."

chapter

13

TUESDAY morning Adrian rapped on January's office door and strode in. "I've got an assignment for you."

January groaned. "I can't even finish the one I'm on."

"Never mind. You'll like this one. You're going away again."

"Adrian, I just got home."

"You're ready," he said. "You've had four days to yourself plus the weekend."

The weekend had gone by uneventfully with no word from Lance to anyone as far as she knew. Monday, Kim had called. She said she'd talked to Teri, there'd obviously been a major misunderstanding, and she apologized. She also hadn't heard from Lance, she said. No one knew where he was or what he was doing. She laughed over the telephone. "He sure can elude the press when he wants. He'll turn up whenever he's ready. Meanwhile, we're all rooting for you."

"You are?" January said with surprise.

"Sure," Kim said. She chuckled. "You two are a perfect match. You are either going to make life totally impossible for each other or else absolutely wonderful. Besides, you have a lot in common. At least according to Lance. He never stopped talking about you around me, you know. How you liked the same kind of art and music and liked to go to galleries together—all the things I can't stand."

January didn't know what to say.

"Anyway," said Kim, "when he does resurface, we'll see if we can get him to overcome his pride a little and give you a call."

"That'd be nice," January said, feeling even more a fool than ever. Her heart was racing but her words came out casual beyond belief.

Kim laughed again. "Can't fool me, girl. You're as gone on him as he is on you. How about lunch some time next week? We have a lot to talk about."

"I'd like that," said January, and she meant it.

For a moment after she hung up she felt a surge of optimism, but almost immediately it left her.

Maybe everyone was rooting for her as Kim said, but somewhere inside herself she was pretty well resigned to the impossibility of the situation. Kim talked as if she and Lance were going to get together. January, as much as she wanted to believe otherwise, was sure it wasn't so. As comfortable and easy as things had sometimes been between Lance and her, circumstances seemed to contrive to work against them.

Circumstances and her own prejudices, she had to admit. For the longest time she had been convinced that Lance was one more womanizing musician. And trust— he'd told her time and again—was so important to him. She winced. Trust was just as important to her and it had been one thing she hadn't been able to give, only to receive! Would Lance be able to forgive her? She doubted it. In fact, she doubted he'd even call.

As she'd done so many times before, she told herself to forget him, not even think about him. Diligently, she applied herself to her work. But her work, which always before had been her release, now proved an obstacle. Try as she might, she still couldn't write the final piece on the tour, and *Offbeat* would be going to press in three days. As yet there was no cover story.

She had been mulling over how to handle it, what exactly was the right approach, when Adrian had come in.

"What kind of an assignment?" she asked.

"You're going to Hawaii for three weeks."

"I'm what?"

"I want you to check out the music scene. I've heard there are a bunch of new groups down there, good ones. See who's playing what and where. Go round to the clubs. I've got Helen typing up a list right now of ones we've already heard about. Check them first, then move on. And you might go around to some of the galleries as well, especially on the main island. See what the art scene is about. Supposedly lots of things are going on— holistic medicine, healing, the works. Cover it all. I want a feature story on Hawaii."

"Adrian, I haven't been home a week. I need some time. I haven't even finished the story on L.A. Express-way."

"Finish it down there," he said, shoving an envelope at her.

She opened it. "Adrian, this is for tonight," she wailed.

"That's right. Seven o'clock flight."

She stared at the ticket in dismay. "I can't. I need time. I have to finish this article. I want to spend more time at home. I've been on the road for three weeks— I'm not ready to go away again."

Adrian folded his arms across his chest and stared at her. "Woman, you amaze me. Every reporter on my staff would beg for this assignment and you are attempting to turn it down. Sun, sea, Hawaii . . . and you don't want to go." He shook his head. "Tell me, has your hesitation anything to do with Lance Devlin?"

"Nothing at all," she muttered. swinging her chair to face the window so he wouldn't see her blush. It had a lot to do with Lance Devlin, although she didn't want to admit it even to herself.

"What are your intentions?" said Adrian. "To sit around at home, glued to the phone, praying for a call— even though you're convinced he's in love with Kim?"

"I'm not so convinced anymore," she said.

"Well, that's a start. However, I don't plan to indulge your moping. You work for me and while you work for me you're going to take the assignments I hand you. Otherwise, you can find yourself another job."

January turned around and looked at him. "You're serious, aren't you?"

"Damn right I'm serious. If Lance Devlin wants to get in touch with you, he will. If he doesn't reach you at home after a while, he'll call here. We'll tell him where you are. Meanwhile I want you out of here. The atmosphere around you is positively morbid."

"Is it that bad?"

"It is," said Adrian. "So go to Hawaii, do a good job, and have a good time. Alicia will be picking you up at five-thirty at home to take you to the airport, so you better go home now and get packed."

"What about my final article on Lance? It's not done yet and you need it in three days."

"You'll write the story there and phone it to me. I know you. You'll have the whole flight to think it over and come up with something. You can do it."

"I guess," said January. She knew she should be excited about the prospect of this trip, that it was probably just what she needed. Normally she would have been elated, not only because of going to Hawaii, but also because scouting out new talent, being the first to see it and report on it, was her forte and one of her favorite things to do. All she could think of, however, was that, as usual, circumstances were contriving to keep her and Lance apart. It's not meant to be, she told herself desolately, knowing sooner or later she was going have to accept it. The smile she put on her face for Adrian felt more like a grimace.

"Hey," he said, "I'm not sending you to your doom."

"I know," she said, clearing her desk and putting her notes for the tour article into a folder. "I'm sure I'll be more enthusiastic once I'm on the plane." She snapped her briefcase shut. "Sorry I can't feel it now. Anyway, I promise you that one way or another you will have your story on Lance within the next twenty-four hours. At least I may be able to get a little perspective."

Adrian smiled. "Yes, you will. And I know I'll have the article. I'm not worried about it." He laughed. "Now get going."

After that things went so fast it seemed that one minute she was leaving the office, the next she was being driven to Honolulu's famed Royal Hawaiian Hotel with its lovely gardens, long pink carpets, and bar on the beach.

Adrian was really giving her the treatment this time, she thought, but after three weeks on the road and only a brief time at home, the luxury was quite deserved . . . and irresistible anyway. It was after ten when she arrived, Hawaiian time, and having eaten on the plane, she decided to go to sleep early that night. Besides, tomorrow the story on Lance had to be written, and despite Adrian's predictions, she felt incapable of doing it.

She gasped with pleasure as she was let into her room overlooking the sea. It was filled with tropical flowers of every color, their scent heady and dizzying. On the dresser, in a bucket of ice, was a bottle of champagne. Adrian's lost his mind, thought January. Certainly he had to be the one responsible. The hotel couldn't possibly do this for every guest.

It wasn't until she was changing for bed that she noticed that one of the large vases of flowers filled with a beautiful magenta flower she'd never seen before had a card on it. She detached it and opened the envelope.

Inside was a plain white card on which was simply written: "Rumor has it that in Hawaii there are diamonds in the sea." She stared at it for a long time. It seemed a strange note for Adrian to attach. At first it seemed an unpleasant reminder of the fiasco with Lance. Then she thought maybe he meant it to say that down here she might find romance—even love. Good old Adrian, she thought with a tender smile. He never quit. But what he didn't seem to realize was that she had already found love and it hadn't worked out. And as she tried to fall asleep the sweet smell of the sea, the rustle of palms beyond her open window, and the delicate perfume of flowers made her miserable. She ached all over, wanting Lance with every fiber of her being. She knew now that life would never be complete without him. He was the other half that made her whole.

Suddenly there was a rapping on her door. She sat up in bed, reached for her long white robe, drew it around her, and belted it. "Just a minute," she called, a little apprehensive. "Who is it?"

"Room service, ma'am."

"I didn't order anything," she started to say as the cart was pushed in, the scent of pork and fresh pineapple wafting deliciously up to her; but she stopped mid-sentence. The person in front of her with green eyes and a dark tan was no hotel employee. The faded jeans and the black T-shirt were not the uniform of a waiter. And the mischievous, devil-may-care grin could belong only to one person.

"Lance!" January said with a gasp.

"Midnight supper, lady," he said, pushing past her. "Where do you want this?"

"Lance," said January, wishing her heart would slow down and that she'd stop shaking. "What are you doing here?"

"Oh, I quit the music business," he said. "I thought it was time I got a respectable job."

"Lance," she said a third time, and then didn't know what to say next.

"Yes?" he said, walking over to her.

"Hold me," she said. "I think I'm about to fall down."

He put his arms around her. "Better?"

"Much." She drew back. "You plotted this whole thing, didn't you?"

He nodded. "Where's that bottle of champagne I had them put in here? You drink it already?"

January laughed. "It's . . . it's there. In the ice bucket."

"Great. Champagne for a celebration!" He got the bottle and uncorked it, sending a white spray across the room. He poured them each a glass and handed her one. He held his up. "To us," he said.

January hesitated. "Are you sure?"

Lance said softly, "Sure as I've ever been of anything."

"To us, then," January said, sipping the champagne. There were tears in her eyes.

Lance took the glass away from her and kissed her gently. "Crying again, are you?"

She nodded happily. "Is this really happening?"

"It's really happening."

"But how . . ."

"Questions later," Lance said, pulling her close. "Much later." He drew her to the bed, kissing her lips, her eyes, her ears, her neck. "I love you," he kept murmuring. "I love you, January, I love you."

His words, his hands, his mouth seemed to possess her. There was nothing in the world but Lance, his body taking hers, her giving herself to him in total abandonment and a delirium of the senses.

After they made love, he held her very close against the length of his body, smoothing the hair off her face, kissing her delicately. "I want to marry you," he said.

She opened her eyes. "What?"

"I want to marry you."

She felt something steel up inside her, tighten into a hard knot. She shook her head. "I can't."

"Do you love me?"

"Yes, I love you. You know I do. I think I did when

I first saw your picture."

"Do you know that I love you?"

January looked into his eyes a long time. "Yes," she said, taking a deep breath. "I know you love me."

"Well, then?"

"Lance, I've been married once."

"You're scared, January, that's all. You were scared when I first touched you and you're scared now. You wanted and loved me right from the beginning and it was the same for me with you. I walked into your office prepared to hate you. Instead I fell in love with you, even though I did everything I could to aggravate you. We love each other, January, and life won't be right for us unless we're together . . . forever. I don't know any other way, except for us to get married."

She was silent, not knowing what to say.

"You're afraid, aren't you? You're afraid I'll do to you what Mike did, afraid I'll leave you or be unfaithful."

She nodded.

"Trust, January. It's everything. My bugaboo—and apparently yours, too. I've realized that at last. You're as hung up on trusting as I. Even if you don't know me well enough yet to know I wouldn't be unfaithful, you've got to trust me."

"I do trust you," said January suddenly. "I've seen you on the road. I know I was the only person you slept with—despite what I thought about Kim. I know you're loyal, I know you're faithful."

"Marry me."

"What about my career?"

"What about it? You can still have it."

"And when you're on the road and I have an assignment that takes me elsewhere?"

"I need a new press agent. I fired Diane. Want the job?"

January smiled. "You know, that's not such a bad idea. The change might be kind of fun. And I could still write my own articles as well." She slapped a hand to her forehead. "Which reminds me, I have one to write on you!"

Lance pinned her down. "Not till you answer my question. Will you marry me?"

"I want children—two of them, at the least!"

"Let's have ten."

"Two will do fine," said January with a grin. "And I don't want a houseful of hangers-on and groupies."

Lance laughed. "No hangers-on, no groupies. You drive a hard bargain, woman. Anything else?"

"No, I think that about covers it."

"Well?" he said.

"Well, what?" she said with a teasing smile.

"What's your answer?"

"I don't know. I have to think about it." She started to roll away from him but he grabbed her around the waist and began to tickle her.

"Stop!" she cried, giggling helplessly. "Stop, please, Lance."

"Not till you say, yes."

"Yes," she cried, "yes, yes, yes."

He pulled away from her and regarded her seriously. "Do you mean it?"

"I mean it," she said, equally seriously. And as she said it, she found the knot of fear finally dissolving, leaving her feeling free and clear and completely happy.

"Your article will have to wait a little longer," Lance said, kissing her again, his hands starting once more to stroke her body which arched up to meet his in an embrace that seemed to go on forever.

Still later, she said, "How did you know I'd be here? How did you arrange all this?"

"This is where I came when I left New York. I've been here a week. I flew down and went into seclusion. I was so angry and hurt by you when you up and left, I didn't know what else to do. I couldn't go back to Los Angeles knowing you were there and assuming you didn't want to see me. So I went into hiding to lick my wounds. A few days ago I called Teri, and then Kim. They told me what had happened—the mixup, your not even realizing what you'd promised."

"A few days ago?" January stared at him. "But Kim said the day before yesterday she didn't know where you were."

"She was lying. As soon as I was sure you really did care about me, I set it up that you'd come here and meet me. It took a lot of deal-making with Adrian. He said the only way he could let you go was if you worked while here. And he was convinced he was going to lose you forever. I assured him he could have your services for at least another month when you got back." Lance grinned.

"It did seem a little weird, his sending me on another assignment so fast." January mused back over the past few days. "Then all these flowers were from you, too."

Lance nodded.

"That explains the card." She gave him a loving smile. "There is one thing I have to tell you, though. There's no such thing as diamonds in the sea. Pearls, yes; diamonds, no."

"Ha," said Lance, "that shows how little you know. Sit up, my sweet, and I will show you diamonds in the sea right outside your window."

They sat up, his arm around her, supporting her.

"Now, look," he said.

She watched as the waves curled up and broke on the beach. As they did, the moonlight glinted off of them and the light playing on the cresting water sparkled and danced and seemed to be a billion dazzling diamonds.

"You're right," she said, and lay her head on his shoulder.

"I'm right about lots of things," he said. "And now you have to get up. You've got an article to write. And while you do it, I'm going to lie in bed and watch you."

"Okay," January agreed, "but do me a favor. Do you have your guitar here?"

"My acoustic guitar."

"Get it, and play for me while I write."

"You got it," Lance said.

She smiled. "Who knows?" she said. "This relationship just might work after all."

"It might," he said, "if you behave yourself."

She grinned. "Not easy for me to do, but I'll try."

A little later she was at the desk, and Lance was sitting cross-legged on the unmade bed drinking champagne and playing his guitar. "I've written the lyric to that new song," he said. "Given it a title, too, of course. It's called 'January in the Middle of the Night.'" He played it for her.

"It's beautiful," she said afterward. She grinned at him wickedly. "Can I use it in my article?"

"Press," he groaned. "What'd you write, anyway?"

January smiled. "Oh, nothing much," she said. "Just a sentimental love story with a happy ending."

There's nothing more precious than your

Second Chance at Love™

_____ 05703-7 **FLAMENCO NIGHTS #1** Susanna Collins

_____ 05637-5 **WINTER LOVE SONG #2**
Meredith Kingston

_____ 05624-3 **THE CHADBOURNE LUCK #3**
Lucia Curzon

_____ 05777-0 **OUT OF A DREAM #4** Jennifer Rose

_____ 05878-5 **GLITTER GIRL #5** Jocelyn Day

_____ 05863-7 **AN ARTFUL LADY #6** Sabina Clark

_____ 05694-4 **EMERALD BAY #7** Winter Ames

_____ 05776-2 **RAPTURE REGAINED #8**
Serena Alexander

_____ 05801-7 **THE CAUTIOUS HEART #9**
Philippa Heywood

_____ 05907-2 **ALOHA YESTERDAY #10**
Meredith Kingston

_____ 05638-3 **MOONFIRE MELODY #11** Lily Bradford

_____ 06132-8 **MEETING WITH THE PAST #12**
Caroline Halter

All of the above titles are $1.75 per copy

✦ Second Chance at Love ✦ ™

All of the above titles are $1.75 per copy

Available at your local bookstore or return this form to:

SECOND CHANCE AT LOVE
The Berkley/Jove Publishing Group
200 Madison Avenue, New York, New York 10016

Please enclose 50¢ for postage and handling for one book, 25¢ each add'l book ($1.25 max.). No cash, CODs or stamps. Total amount enclosed: $_____ in check or money order.

NAME_____

ADDRESS_____

CITY_____ STATE/ZIP_____

Allow six weeks for delivery.   SK-41